A Time to be Tender

SHEILA SEABROOK

DEDICATION

This book is dedicated to the "Name The Book" contest winners.

Meghan Stith, whose entry *A Time to be Tender* is perfect for Mike and Jane's story.

Charline Bonham, whose *Heartbreaker* will be incorporated into the title of book four.

Barbara Watts, whose suggestion *The Defender* is perfect for another series.

Thank you for playing along, ladies, and suggesting such fabulous titles!

DEAR READER

Thank you for picking up a copy of A Time to be Tender, book three in the Rocky Mountain Romance series. I hope you enjoy it.

When I first began to write Mike Toryn's story, I wondered if anyone would fall in love with him or forgive him for what he did to his family in Terms of Surrender. In fact, I told myself I was nuts for even considering the thought of writing his story.

There were moments (or should I say, weeks) that I just wanted to give up. Maybe go get a job at the local library or dollar store. But then I got to the second draft, then the third, and the man had me crying. He was so sweet...heartbroken too...

Of course, now I'm glad I persevered, and I hope you're glad too.

What can I say about my heroine, Jane Watts? I recast her so many times, I lost count. Then I caught a news story and it sparked my imagination. I resisted the idea at first, because it was scary and I didn't know if I could do the character justice. But inevitably, I gave in, and the character and story came together as if Mike and Jane were made for each other.

As they say, true love conquers all.

Until next time, happy reading!

Sheila Seabrook, author of *Always Remember* & *Terms of Surrender*

MORE BOOKS BY SHEILA SEABROOK

Rocky Mountain Romance Series:
Always Remember
Terms of Surrender
A Time to be Tender
Once a Heartbreaker (TBA)
This Time Forever (Sara's Story! TBA)

Caught Between Series:
Caught Between a Lie and True Love
Caught Between an Oops and a Hard Body
Caught Between a Rock and a Hunka Man
Caught Between the Mob and a Hot Cop (TBA)

Novellas:
Wedding Fever (Includes prequel Baby Fever)
The Valentine Grinch
Love Under Construction

It started out as an escape.

Help one sad and lonely widower get his life—and his family—back together again while she hid from her past. But Jane Watts didn't expect to fall for the cowboy next door. Nor did she anticipate he'd fall for her in return.

It was supposed to be an easy out.

The booze, the brawls, the bull riding. But Mike Toryn didn't ask to be saved by his secretive neighbor. Nor did he expect that he would want to save her in return.

What should have been uncomplicated and temporary had suddenly become profound and heartbreaking. And neither Mike nor Jane did heartbreak, not ever again...

A Time to be Tender

CHAPTER ONE

Guilt pressed down on Jane Watts' chest until she couldn't breathe, couldn't think...

...couldn't feel anything but the sorrowful regret that she had somehow survived while everyone else had died. She curled into a tiny ball on the bed and tried to blank her mind, but the memories persisted, refusing to leave her alone.

She'd been warned that the nightmares would continue until she got professional help. But after one visit with the psychologist her sister had recommended, Jane had refused to go back. Rather than talk about her ordeal, she'd decided to spend the rest of her life in seclusion on her parents' southern Alberta ranch.

So on this freezing cold, mid-November morning, when she heard her bedroom door creak open and her mom tiptoe across the hardwood floor toward the window to gently raise the blinds, she sensed her self-imposed exile from the rest of humanity had hit a wall.

"Get up, honey. You're coming with me today."

When she didn't move, there was a huge sigh from the

other side of the blankets, followed by a tug.

Jane had to be quick. Wishing she were five-years-old instead of thirty-two, she grabbed the covers with both hands, dragged them over her head, and held on tight. "Go away. I'm invisible."

"This isn't healthy, Jane—"

"Neither am I," she shot back before her mother, Barbara Watts, could finish whatever she'd been about to say.

"Yes, you are," the older woman stated with another firm yank on Jane's protective shield. "Dr. Kincaid gave you a clean bill of health. Then she gave you another. And just last week, I clearly heard her say those stomach aches you've been having are all in your head—"

"Dr. Kincaid is full of crock," she muttered into the sheets.

"—so honey, there's no excuse to be moping about in bed. Therefore, I'm giving you a choice." Her mother's cajoling voice was closer this time, so close Jane could feel the warmth of her breath against her scalp, so close the subtle fragrance of her chocolate scented body lotion permeated the blankets. "You can either get out of bed and come with me, or head back to Calgary and return to work."

Jane froze. She could barely look her parents in the eyes. How could she face her co-workers and the innocence of her kindergarten students? Surely they would know, just by looking at her, that she was tarnished beyond redemption.

"Well, young lady. What's it going to be?"

Jane pushed back the covers and glared into her mother's lavender eyes. "Can't I take five minutes to regroup?"

"You've had five months. It's time to quit feeling sorry for yourself. You're not the first woman to—"

The room went silent, so silent she could hear the soft swish of her dad shoveling the front drive-pad outside. So quiet she could hear the ice crack on the shutters in the sun and the old farm house creak as the winter frost penetrated deep into the ground.

She sat up, forcing her mother to straighten, and arms crossed, heart breaking into another million pieces, it was all she could do not to scream out in anger. Because if she started, she might never stop. So she kept a lid on her emotions before they spilled free. "I'm not imagining my stomach pain. I'm not making it up, either."

Her mom had left her alone since she'd returned home and allowed her to wallow in the darkness of her pity party. She'd needed to be close to her family. Needed the quiet comfort of the foothills and the nearby Rocky Mountains to patch the broken pieces of herself back together. But apparently the fun times of holing up in bed all day and night, and hiding from the rest of the world were over.

Except she needed more recovery time, like maybe the rest of her lifetime.

Barbara's mouth thinned and she bent to scoop up a blanket off the floor, taking her time to refold it before she set it neatly on the window seat. When she faced Jane again, her calm demeanor was back in place like a Halloween mask that no longer fit. "Jane May Watts, whether or not you like it, you're coming with me this morning."

Arms folded across her chest, Jane stared back at her, determined to be as stubborn as the woman hell bent on dragging her back to the land of the living. But while her mom might only be five-foot-two, the older woman was as feisty and ferocious as an Amazonian warrior.

"Fine," she snapped, sulky and petulant like a teenager high on hormones. "Where are we going?"

"To perform an intervention." Mouth tight, Barbara headed toward the door. "Be down in thirty minutes or I'll sic your father on you."

"Good luck with that," she mumbled, but as her mother disappeared out the door, Jane pushed back the covers and swung her legs over the edge of the bed. As her feet touched the floor, she shivered in the chill of the early morning air and quickly shoved them into the slippers she'd borrowed from her mom.

She rubbed at the spot between her ribcage and breathed deep in an attempt to ease the tightness in her stomach.

It was times like this that she most wished she could draw the line, persuade them all to leave her alone—her mother, her sister, her dad—but she couldn't risk being booted to the curb. And her mom, bless her kind heart, rarely tossed out a threat without following it through.

Her phone bleeped. She picked it up, read the message on the screen, and scowled before she slapped the device face down on the bedside table. Pushing off the bed, she crossed to the window to check out the weather. She passed the remnants of her childhood—4H awards, barrel racing trophies, and a framed photo of her holding her teaching degree on the day she graduated from university—and wished she could be normal again.

Normal and clean and free of the nightmares that continued to haunt her sleep.

That was the worst part of being home. Waking to her parents frightened faces, uncertain what she'd revealed before becoming fully aware that she was safe, healed on the outside, but oh so damaged on the inside.

Reaching the window, she pressed her heated forehead against the icy pane of glass.

Outside, the mid-November sun barely rose above the treetops and cast long shadows along the snow covered ground. Overnight, it had stormed again, and the main yard had been covered with a layer of pristine flakes that sparkled like diamonds in the sunlight. She could see her dad on the driveway, a worn cowboy hat on his head, the snow shovel in his hands, pretending to be oblivious to his youngest daughter's ruin.

But she saw his knowledge in the sloped edges of his shoulders, in the anger in his eyes whenever she accidentally met his gaze, in the new lines on his once unlined face.

Tearing her gaze from his broad back, she let her attention drift past the snow drifts between the house and barn, past the huge round bales of hay wrapped to protect them from the winter moisture, past the cattle dotting the snow covered rolling hills, to the white-capped mountains beyond. Once upon a time, all of this had felt peaceful and safe, but now it seemed like fear permeated every bone in her body.

Jane caught her reflection in the window, and her entire focus shifted to the tiny scar on the edge of her upper lip. The impact pushed her backward, halfway across the room, and stole her breath. She grabbed her chest, felt a hand around her throat—

"*Jane.*"

Her mother's shout broke through the panic squeezing the air from her lungs, and she fell to the floor with a thud.

Footsteps tripped up the steps to the second floor and the bedroom door flew open. "Jane, honey, it's okay.

You're home now. Safe."

She kept her head lowered so the edges of her long hair hid the fear on her face, and pretended to dig through the clothes scattered on the floor nearby.

"I'm fine," she said around the tightness in her throat, unable to cover the high-pitched wobble of her voice. "I'm just looking for something clean to wear."

They'd been through this before and her mother knew the drill. Walk away. Pretend like finding her daughter in a frightened heap on the floor was normal.

Barbara shuffled her feet and cleared her throat. "Breakfast is almost ready. Don't be tardy."

The door closed with a snick behind the older woman, leaving Jane alone to regather her defenses and forcibly turn off the fear while she dug around on the floor for something to wear. Her attention drifted to the bedside table, and on hands and knees, she crawled across the cold floor and opened the bottom drawer.

Below the report cards and teenage diaries were the pills she'd squirreled away. She'd tucked them way in the back of the drawer so no one else would find them, deliverance from the guilt of who she'd become.

God, she missed her old life—the morning rush to get ready for school, the classroom giggles as her five-year-old students settled in for the day. Segregated from everything bad in the world.

But she knew the drill too, and a moment later, she slid the drawer shut, then clambered to her feet on unsteady legs while she clutched a pair of reasonably clean blue jeans, a frayed t-shirt, and a heavy hoodie perfect for the sub-zero temperatures on the prairies.

Jane dressed. Avoiding the mirror, she quickly washed her face, brushed her teeth, and pulled her blonde hair into a ponytail, then headed downstairs. She walked into the kitchen as her mom pulled a tray of freshly baked cinnamon buns out of the oven. "I thought I smelled something delicious."

Barbara pointed to the counter. "Sit. I'll bring you coffee and breakfast in a sec."

"Mom, you don't have to wait on me." She sidled around her mother, grabbed a cup out of the cupboard, and filled it with the dark brew. "Want one?"

"No thanks." Her mom's face elongated, like she'd lost her only friend, and her shoulders hunched as she squeezed the tube of icing over the steaming hot buns with a little more aggression than necessary. "Want the truth, honey?"

Her breath stalled. Surely her mother didn't want to *talk*.

The older woman continued. "I would love a cup of coffee. Dearly, desperately, regrettably. But I won't. As much as it pains me to decline, the delicious brew keeps me awake when I should be fast asleep. I'm now forced to drink herbal tea."

Drawing in a breath, an unfamiliar bubble of laughter worked its way up Jane's throat and escaped as she scooted past her mom again, then sat down on the opposite side of the island to watch her work the tube in her hands. "Herbal tea is good for you, Mom."

"Maybe so, but I miss my coffee."

Five months ago, she'd missed her coffee too…for all of five seconds. Then she'd just missed her freedom and her family. "So where are we going today?"

"To the Rocky Creek Ranch." She paused and glanced up. "You went to school with the owner. Mike Toryn."

Jane sipped at the steaming coffee, relishing the strong aromatic flavor, before setting the cup down to let the dark liquid cool. "I remember Mike. Tall, quiet, cute. Gosh, I haven't thought of him in years."

Barbara set the empty tube in the sink, then bustled across to the fridge to pull out the tray of eggs. "Did you know he was married?"

"Nuhuh," she responded as she caught a melting dollop of icing on the end of her index finger and stuck it into her mouth to suck it off. Her stomach responded with a hungry growl. "Anyone I know?"

"Remember the Davis twins, Hannah and Harley? He married the quiet one. Hannah."

"Sure I remember them." She stole another smidgen of icing. "So what's the problem with Mike and Hannah that you have to go over there and stick your nose into their business?"

Her mom paused and gave her the stink eye. "Helping out a neighbor isn't always interfering in their business. Sometimes it's giving them a helping hand up when they need it the most."

And sometimes, it was just plain, unwanted interference.

Jane blanked her expression and waited for her mother to continue.

As Barbara cracked eggs into a pan, her face elongated. "Hannah passed away last spring. Breast cancer. It was a terrible ordeal for the whole family."

Last spring. In a heartbeat, Jane's appetite vanished. She focused on the cup in her hand and felt her mom's gaze on her. "How sad."

"Very," she continued, her tone mild. "Mike lost his reason to live and his two motherless girls. The twins have been staying with their aunt and uncle, but they need their father. He needs them too, or he will never heal properly."

She toyed with the edge of her mug. "Sounds like a job for Abby, not you."

"Don't even mention Mike around your sister. The girl has it in for that man." She sighed heavily as she whisked the eggs. "Honey, Mike deserves our help. He looked after Hannah and their twins the entire time without any help. Do you know what that kind of pressure does to a person?"

"I suppose." Still, that wasn't any reason to drag her into the mess. She chewed at a jagged fingernail and wondered how she could get out of being dragged along. Because once her mom decided to do something, nothing short of a freight train could stop her. "Why do I have to come?"

"Because that's what neighbors here do. They help each other out. Have you been gone so long you've forgotten?"

She sat up straight, hope stirring in her chest. "Well, technically I don't actually live here, so I'm not really a neighbor."

Barbara stopped stirring the eggs in the pan and eyeballed her with a fierceness that made Jane feel thirteen again. "Five months you've been up in that room. I'd call that living here."

"Fine," she snorted and slouched onto the countertop, one arm supporting her upper body while she spooned sugar into her coffee. "If Mike needed help so bad, why didn't all of you good neighbors help him out then?"

"Because Hannah didn't want anyone to know about her illness. By the time we found out, it was too late and we were attending her funeral." Her mother dumped the eggs onto a plate with some orange slices, then turned like a waitress in a diner and set the plate in front of her. "Eat, honey. All of it. You've gotten so thin and I worry about you."

"Yes, Ma'am." Watching her mom bustle around the kitchen tidying things up, Jane dug in despite the fact that she had no appetite, no will to live, and no wish to leave the house. There had to be a way. Maybe she could fake one of those stomachaches.

The plate vanished from under her nose, and only then did she realize that she'd actually eaten everything on it. While her mom rinsed off the plate and set it in the dishwasher, Jane slid off the stool and rubbed her stomach.

Her mom straightened her back and pointed a spatula at her. "Don't you dare, young lady."

Jane couldn't help it, she smirked. "You're still pretty sharp for an old lady, aren't you?"

"I'm not as old as some and sharper than most, and don't you forget it." She pointed toward the back porch. "Now, go get your boots and jacket on, and we'll get going."

"Okay, but I really think you should call Abby. This is her area of expertise."

Despite her objections, Jane headed to the porch, pulled on her winter jacket and boots, then followed her mom outside. Her dad had the truck warmed up and ready to go. "Morning, Dad."

His troubled blue eyes swept over her. "So you finally came out of your room."

"Yep." She kissed him on the cheek and gave him a hopeful smile. "I don't suppose you could persuade Mom to drive away without me?"

He pulled open the passenger door. "Annoy your mother deliberately?"

On the opposite side of the truck, the door swung open, and Barbara climbed in behind the steering wheel. "Your father knows better than to upset the woman who feeds him." She glanced at her husband. "Are you sure you don't want to come?"

He shook his head. "Positive. This kind of business is best left to you women."

As Jane opened her mouth to protest, her mom said, "This shouldn't take long. We'll be back in time for coffee."

And then her dad closed the truck door and stepped back from the vehicle.

Jane pulled on her seatbelt and glared at her mom. "That's totally unfair."

"What is?" Barbara asked as she navigated the truck backwards down the driveway and turned it down the lane.

"*This kind of business is best left to you women,*" she repeated. "I can't believe Dad allows you to deal with a potentially dangerous situation without his backup."

"First off," Barbara sniffed indignantly. "Your father doesn't *allow* me to do anything. We have an agreement. I do whatever I want, and he gets my permission before he does whatever *he* wants."

"Still, it's not fair," she mumbled while fear twisted her stomach into a ball of pain. She rubbed at the spot between her ribs and mumbled, "I don't feel very good."

Her mother turned the truck off the lane onto the secondary highway and headed south. "And you never will if you don't get out of the house."

Barbara flicked on the radio. As an unfamiliar country tune filled the cab, Jane slumped on the seat, stared out the side window, and wondered if her mother expected her to be the muscle in this operation.

Probably not. The other woman didn't have a mean or spiteful bone in her body.

Yet ten minutes down the road, as the truck steered off

the pavement and drove under the arched gateway with the Rocky Creek Ranch sign on top, Jane still couldn't fathom the reason for her presence.

She finally broke the silence. "So what's wrong with Mike?"

Without taking her eyes off the unplowed road, Barbara sighed. "The boy doesn't care whether he lives or dies."

Jane turned her head and pretended to peer out at the passing landscape.

She totally understood how he felt, and even without seeing him, she knew how he'd react to her mother's interference.

It wouldn't be pretty.

Barbara parked the truck near the house, and shutting off the motor, grabbed the door handle and resumed the conversation. "He's probably still in the bunkhouse sleeping off last night's binge."

Frowning, Jane climbed out of the truck and followed her mom up the porch steps where the older woman peered through one of the windows. "Why isn't he living in the house?"

"He hasn't been, not since last June when the incident happened."

Jane craned her neck to see inside. "Incident?"

She took in the rectangle stack of empty beer cans in the corner of the dining area. Clothes from the laundry room were scattered down the hallway. Unwashed dishes were stacked on the table, countertop, and sink.

"He wasn't always like this, you know, drowning himself in pity and booze." Barbara turned away from the window, retraced her steps through the snow, then headed across the yard toward one of the outer buildings. "Mike loved being a husband and father. He was crazy in love with Hannah, and his life revolved around her and the twins. But when Hannah died, he fell apart. Attacked his sister-in-law. Lost custody of his daughters. They say a person's true colors come out during times of extreme pressure. But that wasn't Mike. It was the alcohol." She huffed out an angry breath. "I've been staying out of his way for months now, but the boy isn't getting any better. There's only one way to deal with him and that's head on."

The fear Jane had battled on the ten minute drive turned into full-fledged terror. She sprinted after her mom, tried to grab her arm, but the older woman was wily and faster than she looked. "Mom, you can't go barging in there."

"No? Just watch me, honey."

As her mom headed straight for the bunkhouse door, Jane stopped to peer through one of the windows.

The man they'd come to roust lay face down on the single bed, the sheets tangled around his hips and legs, his naked back golden from the hours he'd obviously spent outdoors in the summer sun. An empty whiskey bottle had fallen on the floor beside the bed with the cowboy's hand still gripped around it.

Once her mom roused him, they'd be faced with a half naked angry man.

From around the corner, she heard her mom pound on the wooden door and yell, "Mike Toryn, I'm sick and tired of your BS. Get out of bed, or I'll come in there and make you."

Jane ripped her gaze from the broad shoulders and smooth back, and tried to move her suddenly leaden feet, but her fear became a living, clawing animal, and there was no way she could escape its clutches. She fell to her knees and curled into a tiny ball.

The nightmares that plagued her were about to come

true…for the second time in her life.

CHAPTER TWO

The pound of a fist against the solid wood door of the bunkhouse reverberated through Mike Toryn's head like a bullet ricocheting around his brain. Rolling onto his stomach, he stuffed the pillow over his head, burrowed deeper under the covers to escape the early morning chill, and attempted to ignore the intruder at the door.

He'd been dreaming of his beautiful wife holding their precious babies in her arms, love in her gaze, tenderness in her touch, sweetness in her smile. The memory filled his heart with warmth and joy and the treasure of her love…

…until the snick of the door latch, the icy chill of the mid-November air, and the angry tread of footsteps dragged him reluctantly from the dream back to reality. Before his sluggish brain could react, the blankets were ripped off his body and Barbara Watt's familiar voice cut through the fuzziness in his brain.

"Get your butt out of bed, young man, or I'll make you."

He burrowed deeper under the pillow and fumbled blindly for the sheets. "Leave me alone."

The clomp of her winter boots echoed across the floor as she headed in the direction of the bathroom. There was a rush of water from the tap, followed by the return of footsteps, then the sheets, along with the pillow, vanished again.

Ice-cold water hit him square on the head, and splashed across his shoulders and back. He yelped, shot out of bed, and barely avoided knocking his neighbor onto her ass. "What the hell, Barbara?"

"Don't you *what the hell* me, young man." His normally kind neighbor eyeballed him with anger in her eyes and something else. Something that made Mike wish he could turn back the clock and fix everything he'd ruined. "What are you doing, young man?"

"Thanks to you, I'm air-drying," he retorted.

As he stood there shivering, water dripping onto the floor, he forced himself to rein in his temper. No good ever came from anger and he, better than anyone else, knew that for a fact. With a muttered curse, he swiped the water from his face, grabbed the wet sheet off the bed to cover his lower body, then stalked toward the open doorway, slamming it closed to shut out the frigid winter temperature.

Guilt wormed its way into the numbness of his heart, but he shoved it aside, refusing to roll over and allow her to decimate his solitude. His rusty voice came out laced with sarcasm. "Why don't you go pester Walter instead?"

"I don't need to pester Walter. He's up before the sun, taking care of his chores." The glower on her round face deepened and he followed her gaze around the bunkhouse, felt his face heat. It looked like a pig-stye, dirty clothes strewn everywhere, empty beer cans and whiskey bottles scattered like dead soldiers around the room. When she finally turned back to him, her eyes were hard like chips of ice in a tumbler. "Plus, he would *never* abandon his family."

The pain he'd been carrying deep inside hit him square in the solar plexus and sucked the air from his lungs.

"Wow, Barbara, why don't you just give it to me straight?" He gripped the sheet so he wouldn't be tempted to put his fist through the wall and frighten her, and his pain spilled out of his mouth before he could swallow it back. "Don't you think I know how badly I screwed up? Don't you think I know I failed my wife and my girls? Don't you think I regret what I did every moment that I'm awake?"

She didn't take pity on him or pull any punches. "You need more than my help, but until you can admit it, you're stuck with me prodding and pushing you to get sober. Do you want your daughters back or not?"

He didn't deserve to have his girls back, but every day without them made him feel further from his wife and closer to damnation.

Gritting his teeth before he did something stupid—like maybe start bawling like a baby girl—he stalked to the bathroom, grabbed the big fluffy towel his wife had loved so much, and came face to face with the hollow-eyed, gaunt faced stranger in the mirror.

The man staring back at him looked a hundred years old. Dark, puffy circles underscored the haunted dullness of his eyes. He hadn't shaved for weeks, and the straggly beard made him look lost and homeless.

Filled with never ending sorrow, he bowed his head. *Hannah, why did you leave me?*

As the cold penetrated his body and a shiver washed through him, he brought the towel to his face and inhaled, only to discover that the scent of his sweet wife had dissipated. Fighting back tears, he scrubbed the towel over his dripping wet hair and blew out a breath.

Nothing in life had prepared him for a loss of this magnitude. He'd failed his wife, failed his daughters, and nothing anyone could do or say would save him.

Mike turned his back on the pathetic excuse staring back at him in the mirror, and stalked out of the bathroom. Choosing to ignore the stubborn woman standing in his way, he weaved around her and headed toward the bed where he tore off the wet sheets.

"Mike Toryn, you're going to get shaved and showered, and then with my help, you're going to get your life back."

He tossed the towel that now only stunk of his own sweat and despair into the corner with the bed sheets, shouldered his way past her, grabbed a blanket off a chair, and wrapped it around his shoulders, then went to the thermostat to turn up the heat. "The girls are better off with Gage and Harley. Everyone knows it."

A tiny voice inside tried to interrupt, but he silenced it out of habit and squared off against his neighbor. She was motherly and kind and well meaning, and fiercely protective of the ones she loved. There was only one way to get rid of her.

Feeling mean and hung-over from whatever he'd poured down his throat last night, he pinched the bridge of his nose, pride and sorrow mingling into a maelstrom of pain. "I don't need your help, Barbara. I'm doing fine on my own."

"Fine?" She huffed out an angry sigh and kicked at a bundle of dirty clothes on the floor. "You're drinking is out of hand. You hide out here on the ranch except when you make an appearance on the rodeo circuit or the bar looking for a fight. It's time someone helped you find your way back to the land of the living."

The universe had screwed up when it robbed his children of their mother instead of their father. He blew out an angry breath. "It should have been me that died, not Hannah. Everyone knows that, even if they don't want to admit it out loud."

Silence greeted his outburst and he wished he could take back his words. He turned his back on her and began to sort through the pile of clothes on the floor looking for something at least halfway clean.

Her soft, motherly tone washed over him. "No one thinks that except you. Your daughters need you. They lost their mother, which means they need their father even more."

His daughters.

Mike knew he was no longer a man capable of getting up in the middle of the night to care for them. By the time he crawled into bed at night, he was so deep into the booze that if they needed him, he wouldn't even hear them.

He shoved his feet into his cowboy boots, then realized he'd forgotten to put on his jeans. He straightened, his jaw so tight, he wondered if it would ever loosen again. He refocused on the intruder and kept his voice deadly quiet. "Vamoose."

The growing trepidation in Barbara's gaze made him feel even meaner. With his tears under control, he kicked off his boots, and grabbed his jeans. He raised one eyebrow, hating her pity, determined to be cocky. "Like I said, I don't need your help. Shut the door on your way out."

She took a deep breath and just like that, just like the kindly neighbor who had welcomed him into the community five years ago when his wife had been pregnant with the twins, her anger melted away.

"Mike, it's been six months. Everyone knows how much you loved Hannah and how much her death hurt you, but you need to move on. If not for your sake, then do it for the girls. They miss you." When he didn't say anything, she sighed and headed toward the door. "You have twenty minutes, young man. Get showered and into some clean clothes. Then move your belongings up to the house, because as God is my witness, you're rejoining the living."

He watched the bossy woman stomp outside, leaving the door open behind her—*again*—leaving him alone with the guilt that washed away the pain.

Mike slammed the door shut and the sound echoed through the room with an explosion that tripled the magnitude of his hangover. With a glower at the pigsty surrounding him, he stalked to the bathroom, took care of morning business, then turned on the water in the shower. He scraped one hand through his dirty beard, and while he waited for the water to warm, he shaved.

He hadn't been up to the house since the incident early last summer when he'd gone off the deep end and attacked his sister-in-law, scaring his daughters into hiding from him as though he'd become a madman. He'd done it once, and because he felt as though he were still on the precipice of going over the edge, he refused to ever put them in that position again.

Mike ripped his gaze from his reflection, stepped into the steaming shower, and stood there while the hot water pounded against his back and soothed some of the ache in his chest.

But the ache never went totally away, and every day it seemed to pull him deeper into its dark abyss of despair.

He turned off the water, climbed out of the shower, and toweled off the moisture, then dug through his clothes for the cleanest of the dirty ones. Tugging on his boots, he pushed off the bed, slammed his cowboy hat on his head, winced as his hangover ricocheted between his eyes, and stepped out of the bunkhouse into the cold. As the sun glinted off fresh fallen snow, its brightness nearly blinding him, he tugged dark glasses out of one pocket and set them on his nose.

Mike took a deep breath to clear his head, and the memory of the scent of his wife's perfume swirled through his brain, causing him to stumble over his well-worn cowboy boots and fall to his knees. He squeezed his eyes shut and remembered how she'd felt in his arms—tiny and precious and breakable—and it was all he could do to swallow back the sob climbing up his throat.

Hannah, baby, are you still here?

She didn't answer...she didn't have to.

Every day, he woke up groggy in his bed and listened for the softness of her breath in his ear, imagined the sweet press of her body wrapped around his.

And every day, the silence and loneliness drew him further into the lonely pit of pain.

Mike swiped his jacket sleeve across his eyes, stumbled back to his feet, and stalked across the yard. Ignoring the throbbing pain in his head, he pulled soft leather gloves onto his hands, secured the ties on his chaps, and focused in on the bullpen.

Cyclone.

His deliverance from the pain of having his wife and family ripped from his life.

All he had to do was get on the bull and if he survived—again—he'd return to the bunkhouse and drown out his memories in the bottom of a whiskey bottle, then try again tomorrow.

Baby, what are you doing?

Startled, Mike opened his eyes.

A woman sat on the top rail of the bullpen, the low winter sun at her back creating a halo-like effect around her body, casting her face into shadows. His wife's name escaped in a single breath. "Hannah?"

She swung one leg over the top rail of the fence and into the bullpen, like a red flag. "Actually, it's Jane. Jane Watts. Barbara's daughter." With the low winter sun shining from behind her, her face was in shadows. "My mom dragged me with her today. I guess she thought she'd need backup." When he didn't immediately say something, she laughed, a short bark that rivaled the rusty sound of his own laughter, and followed it up with some muttering that sounded an awful lot like, "I don't know what she was thinking. It's clear, the woman is a warrior and I am not."

Mike shifted out of the glare of the sun and saw long legs encased in faded blue jeans, winter boots that came halfway to her knees, a lightweight jacket with a hoodie covering her head, and beneath the hoodie, she wore a black toque. Blonde tendrils of hair escaped, framing her face, elongating the oval shape, casting shadows in the hollows of her cheeks.

But it was her eyes that arrested him. Beneath the soft purple hues that reminded him of shared sunsets with his wife, he recognized her pain, and he felt himself fall. Deep and hard and strange because he still loved his wife so much.

Her expression shifted, drawing his gaze from her mesmerizing eyes, and her mouth stretched into a semblance of a smile as she hooked a thumb toward the house. "If you're looking for my mother, she's gone to break into your house. I'd apologize for her pushiness, but you look like someone who's accustomed to her poking and prodding into your private life."

Inside the pen, the bull snorted and pawed the snow packed ground, drawing Mike's attention. He glanced from the mean spirited creature to the woman swinging her blue jean clad leg nonchalantly inside the pen, and growled out a warning. "Get out of there before you get yourself killed."

She hopped down, all right, on the inside of the pen. "Were you planning to ride him? He looks *really* dangerous."

There was so much nonchalance in her easy stance that Mike couldn't help but wonder if maybe someone else didn't care whether she lived or died. He took a careful step forward so as not to agitate the bull, and kept his voice low and easy. "He's the meanest bull on the rodeo circuit, sweetheart, and if you don't get your butt out of there fast, he's going to—"

The bull lowered its head and charged.

Trample you.

As Mike leapt for the fence and grabbed onto one rung, ready to sacrifice himself to save the woman from her own stupidity, she scrambled up the other side and landed on her feet in front of him.

The bull crashed against the metal rails, and the angry vibration raced through his hand and up his arm to his shoulder.

Mike gritted his teeth, the whiskey consumption from last night playing havoc with his reflexes and brain cells. He released the metal and turned to face the nonchalant woman in front of him, her hands stuffed into the pockets of her winter jacket, her long legged stance defiant and a whole lot reckless. "Are you *trying* to get yourself killed?"

"Is that what you were going to do?" When he didn't answer, she gave an exaggerated, one-shouldered shrug. "Don't let me stop you. I'm sure Hannah and your girls will forgive you for *that*."

Guilt burned in his gut, up his esophagus, and he thought he'd be sick right there in front of her. But then he clamped down on the heartbreak and pain that dogged his every sober moment, and stepped toward her.

With sudden trepidation, she quickly stepped back, and everything inside of him ground to a halt.

Her frightened expression reminded him of his sister-in-law and his twin daughters, and something inside him shifted. Something that he'd lost the moment that Hannah had died. Something that felt as foreign as having other people in his space.

Compassion.

Mike realized how dangerous he must appear. Nearly a foot taller. Probably twice her weight. He eased back to give her plenty of physical space and gave her a shrug back. "And what were you doing in there? The same thing?"

Mouth trembling, she turned on the heel of one boot and fled toward the house as though she were being chased by a pack of starving, snarling wolves...or a man crazed with grief.

A few moments later, he saw Barbara hustle her into Walter's truck and drive away, leaving him alone once again.

Which was exactly how he liked it.

No kindly neighbors to wake him from dreams of his wife.

No lost souls with bruised eyes and suicidal tendencies.

Just him and his sorrow and guilt.

The tiny voice of his beloved wife infiltrated his thoughts, and he forgot about everything but what he'd lost.

What are you doing, honey?

Mike turned back to the bullpen and glared at the mean beast inside.

What does it look like I'm doing, baby? I don't want to live without you. He gritted his teeth against the anger churning in his gut. *You left me, Hannah, and it turns out I'm not the man you thought I was.*

But our babies—

I'm protecting them the best way I know how.

Then he stalked toward the bullpen and climbed up the fence rungs.

The beast head-butted the steel posts, the force nearly jarring Mike's teeth out of his head. He gave a tug on the brim of his cowboy hat, clamped down on the heartbreak that seemed to dodge his every sober moment, and climbed inside.

CHAPTER THREE

That night, Jane huddled under the covers to stay warm, but every time she closed her eyes to try to sleep, she saw the cowboy standing outside the bull's pen, his expression like stone, his gaze hidden behind the dark sunglasses. Despite the fact that he'd scared her with his tall frame, wide shoulders, and angry stance, she knew she had to go back to check on him.

He'd looked like he needed a friend as badly as she did, and she couldn't help but wonder if he'd climbed on top of that nasty bull and held on until he couldn't anymore. He could be lying in the snow and mud, trampled, barely alive...or worse.

What harm could a little visit do? He wouldn't even have to know she'd been there. She could ride in from the fields, sneak in from behind the horse barn, then stay in the shadows and get out before he caught her. He'd probably be sleeping off another hangover anyway.

Long before daybreak, she heard her parents moving about, their voices hushed while her mom cooked breakfast and her dad made the coffee. There was comfort in their routine, in the fact that some things never changed even when other things changed around them.

As the first hint of daylight hit the bedroom window, her dad left the house, headed toward the horse barn to take care of the morning chores. She heard her mom head into the basement, then the sound of water swishing softly through the plumbing pipes.

Jane rolled out of bed, her eyes scratchy from lack of sleep, and quickly washed and dressed. Determined to sneak out of the house without a parental inquisition, she tiptoed down the staircase and across the hall to the kitchen, trying to remember where every creak in the floor was so she could avoid them. But with her mom's supersonic hearing, she cringed with every squeak of the old farmhouse.

Somehow she made it to the back porch without being caught, and she pulled on her boots, then her jacket, zipping up one tooth at a time. As she turned toward the door, she ran right into the antique coat stand sending it crashing to the floor.

Her mother's voice echoed up the basement stairs. "Walter, is that you? What did you forget?"

Jane considered slipping out without saying a word, but then the older woman would worry about intruders in the house. "It's just me, Mom."

"What are you doing, honey?" Barbara appeared at the bottom of the stairs, then started up when she took in Jane's boots and jacket. "Are you going out?"

She bent to retrieve the stand and set it upright in its place. "Just for an early morning ride."

Barbara stepped into the porch and reached into the closet. "I'll come with you. I could use the exercise."

Jane bit back a wince. Her parents had enough to worry

about without being told that their neighbor might be *dead*. "I'd—um—like to be alone."

As her mom retracted her arm from the closet and let it drop to her side, Jane saw the hurt on her face before she could cover it up. "You have your cell in case you get into trouble?"

Jane patted her jacket pocket. "Right here, Mom. Don't worry about me, okay? I'll be fine." She crossed the porch and gave her mom a hug. Softly, she said, "Text if you want me to check in."

As she pulled back, she caught her mom wiping away a tear. "I love you, Jane Watts."

Jane's throat got thick. "I love you too, Mom."

And giving her mom another hug, she turned and headed out into the fresh fallen snow, crossing the yard to the barn, the snow crunching and packing beneath her feet.

Inside the barn, Walter was spreading fresh straw. "Morning, Dad."

He stopped and leaned on the handle of the pitchfork, his gaze taking in her appearance. "Where are you off to?"

"Just a ride. Want me to stay and help you here instead?"

"No, I have it under control. Are you dressed warm enough?"

Her parents always worried about her, especially these days. "Yes, Daddy, I am."

He glanced toward the stalls. "Pepper could use some exercise. Mind taking her?"

"Sure."

He set aside the pitchfork, and while she led the horse out of the stall, her dad retrieved a currycomb and pick. Jane brushed down Pepper's back and her dad checked the hooves.

They worked in silence, brushing, picking, the soft tones of a Jessie Adams' song playing in the background. Jane cleaned the pad and put it in place while her dad grabbed a saddle and hefted it across the aisle and onto the horse's back. Together they tightened the straps.

As she did up the last tie, she glanced up and found him watching her, concern in the fading blue of his eyes.

She might not believe it—her parents obviously didn't believe it either—but maybe it was time to start acting as if she wasn't frightened every second of the day so that her parents could stop worrying about her.

Quietly, she said, "I'm going to be okay, Dad."

"I know, sweetheart." He brushed at his eyes, then cupped his hands together and bent forward slightly. "Up you go."

Jane put her foot on his hands and swung up onto the saddle. As her dad backed out of the way, she gave him a smile. "I have my cell so I can check in with Mom."

"Good." He slapped the horse gently on the hindquarter, and with a smile and wave, Jane rode out of the barn.

It was cold and crisp and sunny, and as Jane rode south and crossed the boundary from her parents' property onto the Rocky Creek Ranch, trepidation set in. She reined Pepper in and started to urge him around before she stopped herself.

The problem was, she didn't know the cowboy very well. It had been fifteen years since they'd gone to school together. But her parents seemed to like him and they were usually a good judge of character.

Still, she'd trusted a stranger once and—

Before she chickened out, she pulled out her cell phone, tugged off one mitt, then thumbed the screen as she texted her mom. *Over at the Rocky Creek Ranch for a bit. Everything is a-ok with me.*

Thx for letting me know, honey. Give Mike what for from me.

Right, like she'd do that. She tucked the phone back into her pocket, then reined Pepper around, gave him a nudge in the flanks with her heels, and as he broke into a trot, they continued south.

By the time she reached the trees behind the barn, the chill in the air had started to creep through her jacket and the layers she wore beneath. She tied the reins to a tree, then giving the horse a pat on the flank, she ducked out of the obscurity of the trees and raced to the bunkhouse where she straightened and peered through the window.

Empty.

The bed appeared as rumpled as yesterday. It was obvious he'd changed the wet sheets—he'd probably done that before he climbed back into it—so she changed direction and weaved her way across the yard toward the bull pen.

It was empty, neither bull nor cowboy in sight. Not even a cowboy hat ground into the mud.

She tugged at the collar of her jacket, sweating now, and saw the small door leading into the horse barn open. As she peered in through a window, still not seeing him, she heard a crunch of snow behind her.

"Can I help you with something?"

Her breath catching in her throat, she forced herself to turn around and face him. "I—uh—good morning. I was—um—checking to see if you were still alive."

He quirked one masculine brow. "And I wouldn't be because…?"

The question hung in the air between them. She

suddenly felt stupid, like she'd imagined his grief to be more than what it was. "Uh—yeah—you know. The booze. The bull. The idiot potentially on top."

"Ah." There was a barely noticeable relaxation of his wide shoulders, which looked broader under the winter coat he wore. Broader and scarier and more dangerous than yesterday when she'd been here with her mother. She backed up a step, started to shiver uncontrollably, and he frowned across the distance separating them.

"Are you cold?"

"I-I-I'm f-f-fine," she stuttered which clearly showed she wasn't fine at all. She shoved her hands into the jacket pockets and backed up some more, straight into the wall of the building, suddenly flustered and afraid. "If you'll move out of my way, I'll—I'll uh—I'll be on m-m-my—"

He moved, and she squeaked and shut her eyes and cowered against the building, covering her head with her arms, waiting for the power of his fist to take her down.

Her heart thumped hard, then harder still as a heartbeat passed. Then another.

Then still another.

"Jane?"

Too afraid to lower her arms, she tried to peek through the opening between her jacket sleeves, but the only thing within her line of vision was a bank of plowed snow.

"*What?*" she breathed, and it came out as little more than a puff of frosty air and a squeak.

"Put down your arms and open your eyes, Jane."

Patience laced his voice, so much patience that she shifted, rotating the upper half of her body till she located him several feet away. It registered that he'd moved farther away, not closer, and she suddenly felt foolish. Embarrassment heated her from the inside out.

She lowered her arms, straightened, and eyeballed him. "My parents know I'm here."

"Good." He turned and angled toward the open door of the barn, his very large hands tucked into the pockets of his coat, his body language easy, the tone of his voice nonchalant. "Run away if you wish, but if your parents find you frozen half way home and try to blame me, I'll tell them that their daughter is an idiot."

Her words from yesterday...sort of.

The unreasonable fear inside began to unfold. Because she couldn't stop shivering, because she knew he was totally right and the last thing she needed on the ride home was a case of hypothermia, she reluctantly followed him.

And just like that, Jane remembered that the man was still grieving for his wife. He wasn't a serial killer. In fact, *she* was probably the most dangerous thing here at this moment, likely to go ballistic if he made a move toward her again.

As she walked through the open door, she pulled her hands out of her pockets and paused to let her eyes adjust to the florescent lights.

His voice came from quite a distance away. "I'm surprised Barbara didn't come with you."

Jane squinted and stepped cautiously further into the warmth. "Well, I didn't intend to come this way, but after yesterday and the bull—"

His haunted gaze met hers only briefly, and when he looked away, she involuntarily closed the distance between them. He stood in front of a saddle stand, a cloth in his hand, and rubbed oil into the saddle. "As you can see, I didn't kill myself."

"Good thing." A bubble of laughter tried to escape and she swallowed it back before he got the impression that she was being rude. "I would have hated to scrape your pretty cowboy hat out of the mud and toss it into the garbage."

Something in his demeanor relaxed, but he still appeared stiff and unwelcoming. Feeling slightly braver, she wandered closer, then noticed that he had a new bruise on his rather handsome face. She decided not to mention it. "I'm sorry about Hannah. I just found out yesterday."

His jaw clenched and his hand tightened around the cloth. "All the apologies in the world won't bring her back."

Jane stopped right in the middle of the aisle, fear blooming inside her chest, sucking the air from her lungs and the stiffness from her legs.

"I know, and I'm still sorry." Surprisingly, his hand in a fist didn't make her rear back and run this time, and she wondered if this was an indication that she was finally getting better. As the warmth of the stables began to seep through her jacket, she unzipped it. "Do you have another cloth?"

The edge of his unsmiling mouth ticked up. "You really must be bored."

As he reached past her for a rag, she stepped back to avoid contact, then inhaled the scent of man and horse. The combination sent a swirl of something wicked spirally through her and she pushed it away.

Jane took the cloth from his outstretched hand, and as she rubbed oil onto the opposite side of the saddle, she found herself saying, "I get how hard it is to lose someone you care about deeply." God, how she got it, even though she hadn't known the others personally. When tears threatened, she forced a laugh. She could feel his gaze on her, but she wouldn't look at him. "So maybe you wouldn't mind if I hung out here once in a while. I promise not to talk about your loss if you promise not to ask me questions about…me."

His voice was gruff and thick. "Two sad people trying not to make each other sadder?"

She glanced up at him, the tightness in her stomach easing a bit more, and grinned. "Yeah. You can talk about bull riding and I'll talk about—"

In that instant, she realized that she had nothing in her life to talk about that wouldn't lead directly back to the nightmare she wanted to forget. She shrugged. "Well, maybe I'll ask questions and let you do all the talking. Men are notorious for their chattiness."

He laughed again, this one less rusty than the first, and she met his gaze, saw the quiet humor in his eyes, the kindness on his face.

It made her heart swell with happiness that she had eased his sorrow, if only for a few seconds, and she tucked the memory away for later when she was alone in her bed and too frightened to close her eyes.

The barn door whispered open, and a woman with cinnamon hair and startling emerald eyes stepped inside. A tall, hunky cowboy followed her in and shut the cold out behind them. They looked like—

Jane's eyes widened, and she forgot all about her fear of strange men. Without taking her gaze off the couple, she reached over the saddle and grabbed a handful of Mike's jacket. "Is that who I think it is?"

She felt the shrug of his shoulder in the movement of his arm.

"Depends on who you think it is."

Jane released him, skittered around to the other side of the saddle to stand shoulder to shoulder with him, and tried not to shriek. "I'm her biggest fan."

"Well, in that case," he drawled, which drew her attention to his face. He grinned down at her, his eyes crinkled at the corners, gold flecks sparkling within the green depths. And she was caught up in his attractiveness, how his eyes were addictively filled with laughter, almost making her forget about the couple headed their way. "Would you like an introduction?"

"Yes, please," she breathed as she refocused on country western superstar Jessie Adams and her hunky husband.

CHAPTER FOUR

Mike couldn't help but notice that Jane's fear and trepidation had vanished in the presence of his celebrity guests, and he wondered what had happened to make her so afraid.

Better not to wonder, he decided as he started to turn away, because curiosity always led to questions, and questions always led to familiarity. And familiarity meant getting to know someone and letting them into his life.

Yet as her eyes continued to widen, and her jaw grew slack with awe, he found himself smiling down at her profile.

The smile felt strange, as out of place as the rumble of laughter that had escaped seconds ago, and it faded just as quickly. But the awestruck expression washed away the last of her fear, and changed her expression from pinched to beautiful.

A fact that he shouldn't be noticing. It made him feel awkward and deceitful, like he was betraying his wife and his marriage.

Mike clamped down on the urge to bolt and turned his

A TIME TO BE TENDER

focus away from her to make introductions. "Jess, Nate, this is Walter and Barbara Watts' youngest daughter, Jane."

Jane jumped to life, grabbing Jessie's hand and pumping it. "Oh my god, I can't believe you're actually here. I've been listening to your music since the beginning, Ms. Adams."

Jessie's cheeks flushed, almost as though it wasn't every day that a fan gushed about her music. Although since her marriage, she'd cut her touring hours way back, so maybe she wasn't accustomed to it anymore.

"Please, call me Jessie." She steered Jane around. "This is my husband, Nate Coltrane."

Jane was now pumping his hand for all she was worth. "I know. I saw you both in the newspapers, People magazine. Entertainment Tonight. *Everywhere*. I'm thrilled to meet you in person."

As she continued to pump the other man's hand, and looked like she wasn't about to stop, Mike covered her hand with his own and dislodged her grip. "So what brings you two out here this morning?"

The couple in front of him exchanged an uncomfortable glance. Then with a quick glance at Jane, Nate replied. "We should probably discuss this in private."

"Oh." Jane stepped back into Mike, then quickly skittered to the side. "Oh. I'll just get out of your way."

But Mike had seen the loneliness on her face, and for some reason, he didn't want to let her go. He stilled her departure with a touch to the arm, then took a not so wild guess. "Is this an intervention?"

Jessie's lips thinned and she gave a sharp nod.

He released the woman at his side before she turned back into the fearful creature he'd seen outside. "Whatever you have to say, you can say it in front of Jane. We have no secrets."

He felt Jane's eyes on his face, could sense her unspoken question. *We don't?*

The couple exchanged a look, then Nate shifted, clearly uncomfortable about where the conversation was headed. "We thought you should know. Lisa has started to call Harley mommy."

And just like that, everything in Mike screeched to a halt. Before anyone could see his pain, he started to oil the saddle again. As the silence stretched out, he realized they were waiting for him to say something. He cleared the pain from his heart and the emotion from his voice, and attempted to be rational. "When you think about it, except for their hair cut, Hannah and Harley looked exactly the same."

He'd confused them too, early last summer when he'd gone off the deep end and called Harley by her sister's name.

Nate continued. "They're young enough to forget you and Hannah. The twins are asking Gage and Harley to adopt them."

He nodded, as though in agreement with the idea, while the thought of life without them threatened to suck him into a black hole. "Of course. They love their aunt and uncle." Only by sheer force of will did he keep his voice steady and his anger in check. "Why are you telling me this?"

Nate closed the distance between them and put one hand on Mike's shoulder. "Do you think Hannah would want them to forget her?"

The quiet question rocked Mike to his soul and the ever-present urge to cry welled up. At this very moment, he felt like he had when he'd first lost his beautiful wife. As though his heart were being ripped out of his chest and crushed.

Somewhere down the aisle, a pony neighed and the straw rustled under its hooves. Otherwise everything was quiet, as though not a soul were breathing.

As the silence grew, Nate finally spoke. "If you're not careful, bro, you'll lose them forever."

Words rushed up his tight throat and squeezed out of his mouth, quiet and desperate. "I don't know how to be a parent without Hannah. Everything I learned, I learned from her."

Nate's strong voice enveloped him with hope. "Do you think I knew anything about being a dad when I brought Sara home from the hospital?"

Mike raised his head, saw the stricken expression on Jessie's face, and realized the guilt never went away. And he realized that if he didn't do something—if he let his daughters go without a fight—he'd regret it for the rest of his life.

As though sensing his wife's pain, Nate released him and returned to her side, putting one arm around her shoulders and pulling her close. "I had to rely on Sam and Maude, and eventually I sort of figured things out. I won't lie. It wasn't easy. There were plenty of days and nights when I wanted to give her to someone who wasn't as screwed up as I was." He exhaled a sigh. "You have friends and family who love you and want to see you happy, Mike. Let us help. Let us in."

When he didn't reply, Nate continued. "We'll be out of town for a few days. Jess has a charity concert. Maybe by the time we return, you'll be ready to take some action."

As they left, Jane came to stand beside him. She put one hand on his, stopping the circular motion of applying the oil to the saddle.

"He's right," she said quietly. "You can't let that happen or you'll regret it for the rest of your life."

He peered up into her clear mauve eyes. "Do you want to know the truth?"

She nodded. "Always. Remember what you said? We have no secrets."

"The twins are better off with Gage and Harley. Forcing them to return home against their will would be worse than letting my brother and his wife adopt them."

There. He'd spoken the truth as he saw it. He pulled his hand away and tried to stay focused on the saddle instead of the shredding of his soul.

Jane's voice stilled his movements. "But they're your daughters and I can see that you love them with every inch of your being. Don't let one mistake cost you your precious little ones." She grabbed his cell off the counter. "I'm putting my number into your cell. That way when you need someone to talk to, you can call me."

He crumpled the cloth in his hand and tossed it aside. "What about you? Do you have someone to talk to?"

She didn't look at him, and the words rolled off her tongue like a lie. "I don't need anyone to talk to."

Mike let it go for now. He knew that he had to make a choice. Run from his responsibilities like he'd been running since his wife's death. Or man up and raise his girls like Hannah would have wanted him to.

He didn't have a choice. If he continued on as he was, he might as well already be dead.

But if he fought for the girls, if he regained custody and had the privilege of raising them, when he finally joined his wife in the afterlife, she wouldn't hate him for who he'd become and what he'd done.

Once he started, there'd be no turning back.

His gaze settled on the woman entering her phone number into his phone and his number into hers. Her forehead was scrunched in concentration, and for the first time since he'd seen her yesterday, she had color in her cheeks and she didn't seem afraid.

He glanced at her ring finger.

There was no wedding ring or engagement ring...not even an indentation from one recently removed. So what had happened to her and why did it suddenly seem important to find out?

Her cell phone buzzed, and as she handed back his phone and thumbed through the screens on her device, the scrunched look between her eyebrows grew more pronounced. "What's the next move?"

His next move...

As he watched her frown down at the screen and the edges of her mouth turned down, Mike shrugged. "I have to go see Abby."

Her head jerked up. "My sister is your social worker?"

He nodded, suddenly glum. "Want to come watch me beg her to give me my kids back?"

She nodded and chewed on her bottom lip. "You are so lucky I'm here to help you."

But the concerned light in her eyes didn't offer him much hope at all.

Because Abby Watts hated his guts more than anyone else he knew, and he couldn't figure out why.

CHAPTER FIVE

Haunted by the grief and remorse in the cowboy's eyes, Jane tossed and turned all night. She knew the right thing to do was help reunite Mike with his daughters, but the thought of spending so much time with him scared her. Because what if—

The bedside clock rang shrill and loud, startling her awake. She bolted upright in the bed, hands clenched around a heavy quilt, heart pounding, momentarily disorientated. Until the nightmarish vision cleared and she noticed sunlight streaming in the bedroom window, saw her belongings scattered around the room, smelled the scent of bacon in the air.

Her shoulders slumped and her fists unclenched.

She was home, safe, not still locked in that damp, dark, cold metal container. Sprawling back on the bed, she forced herself to breathe deeply until her heartbeat returned to normal and the sweat on her skin dried. As she rolled into a sitting position on the edge of the bed, she pushed the last remnants of the dream out of her head and wondered if the nightmares would ever stop.

Probably not. And now she was stuck alone for the rest of her life because who in their right mind would want to take on a nutcase like her? *She* didn't want to deal with her personal brand of craziness. Why would anyone else?

The scent of bacon accosted her nostrils again and when her stomach grumbled noisily in response, she scrambled into her clothes, unable to remember the last time she'd been this hungry.

Since her return home, her mom had practically had to force feed her which, she supposed, at least gave the older woman something to do besides think about what had happened to her youngest daughter.

Not that her mother's job jar was ever empty. The older woman rarely sat still, and when she did, she'd have either an e-reader or her knitting needles in her hands. She liked to knit baby booties and baby scarves and baby blankets. Anything baby with hopes that one of her daughters would take the hint and get to work making her some grand babies.

Unfortunately, it wasn't likely to happen any time soon unless her sister, Abby, got over her dislike of men.

Jane pushed out of bed and headed into the bathroom to wash her face and comb her hair. This morning, the woman staring back at her from the mirror had a wee bit of color to her cheeks, a result of yesterday's ride in the fresh mountain air.

She headed down the stairs, but when she heard her mom's hushed voice in the kitchen, she stopped in the hallway.

"It should never have happened, Walter. So careless and irresponsible."

"I know, honey, but we can't turn back the clock. You need to let it go."

There were tears in her mom's voice and her dad sounded choked too.

Guilt slammed into Jane's chest and crushed the air from her lungs. She pressed back against the wall, one hand over her mouth to capture the sob before it escaped, eyes squeezed shut to press back the tears.

It *had been* her fault. She *had been* careless. Irresponsible too. If she hadn't trusted so easily…if she'd only stopped to think…if she hadn't taken the ride from a stranger…

There was the sound of tissue being pulled from the box, then her dad's wobbly voice.

"Be strong, Barbara."

"I'm trying, Walter, but it's so damn hard."

Jane decided she had to get out of the house and give her parents some much needed space. She'd been so wrapped up in her own pain, she hadn't noticed how much those around her were hurting too. For the past five months, they'd tiptoed around her like she was a fragile piece of china.

And what had she done for them?

Nothing. And the worst was still to come…

No more. It was time to suck it up and at least pretend that her chest wasn't in a fear-filled vice every second of the day.

Silently, she retreated to the edge of the stairs, tears burning at the back of her eyes and throat. Swallowing back her pain, she coughed loudly before she retraced her steps back down the hallway. With a smile fixed on her face, she strode into the kitchen. "Good morning, all."

Her parents pulled apart, and while her mom turned her back to wipe her eyes and nose, her dad shielded her from view.

Jane stopped in front of him, stretched up to kiss him on the cheek, then said, "I'm just going to grab a coffee and sit on the porch. The sunshine is beautiful today."

Surprise sparked in the faded blue of her dad's worried gaze. "Good idea. I might come join you, if I can persuade your mother to give me the morning off."

Barbara huffed out a wobbly laugh. "In your dreams, Walter."

He moved aside to allow Jane access to her mom. "Your mother is a slave driver."

Jane crossed to her mom, kissed her on the cheek, and gave her a hug around the shoulders. "I know. That job jar never hits empty."

As she headed to the coffee pot, her mom retorted with, "I keep you young, Walter Watts, and you love every second of it."

They were back to kiboshing, which meant everything was normal again, at least on the surface. As she turned from the pot, she looked at her parents—really saw them for the first time since she'd returned home wrecked and damaged. They'd both aged ten years and it was all her fault.

Yes, she needed to pretend to be fine so they could get back to their normal life.

Jane dropped her gaze to the cell phone in her hands and slid open the screen to see her sister's text from yesterday.

Heard you're at the Rocky Creek Ranch. Stay away from that man, sis. He's DANGEROUS.

The only thing dangerous about Mike Toryn was that the man was too attractive. When he laughed—as brief and infrequent as it had been—something sinfully delicious had popped into his gaze before he'd bottled it up and replaced it with grief and guilt.

She raised her gaze and found her parents watching her, and her own guilt barometer spiked.

If Mike blamed himself for the death of his wife and the loss of his twin daughters, he was probably feeling way worse than she did.

She made a decision and straightened from the countertop.

"I'm going into town with Mike today. He's meeting with Abby to discuss custody of the twins and I'd like to be there to offer my support." She huffed out a laugh. "You know how Abby gets. Crazy protective. Maybe if she sees him with me, she'll back off a little."

Barbara tsked as she dabbed at the tears on her eyelashes. "I don't know what's gotten into that girl. How can she keep those sweet little ones away from their daddy?"

Her mom was getting all bristly which meant she was done with the tears...for now anyway.

Walter put one arm around his wife's shoulders. "It's not right. Mike's a good man. A good father too. How did we raise such a mean spirited child?"

To alleviate the growing tension in the room, Jane smiled brightly. "Well, I'll try to help him out. See you all later."

She slipped on her coat and boots, and once she was out on the porch, she texted Mike. *I've decided to come help you.*

His reply came almost immediately. *Forget I asked.*

I can't. Pick me up. You need moral support.

There was silence and she wondered if he was going to ignore her now. Then—

I can handle your sister alone.

She made a face at the screen and wished he could read between the lines. *Fine, then pick me up so I can get away from my parents.*

The seconds ticked by while she waited for his response.

What's wrong with your parents? They're the nicest people I know.

They're too nice, she typed. *That's the problem.*

This time, there was an even longer delay. She sat down on the porch swing. The chill of the wood seeped through her jeans and penetrated her skin.

Finally he responded. *I'll be there in ten. Be ready. Thx.*

Jane tucked the phone into her pocket, downed her coffee, and by the time she reentered the kitchen to rinse out the cup and put it in the dishwasher, her parents were elsewhere. She checked her face in the mirror, tried unsuccessfully to ignore the scar on her lip, grabbed a slice of bacon from the fridge, and pulled the boots back on just as Mike drove into the yard.

Slipping and sliding on the snow and ice, she loped to the truck, climbed into the cab, and gave him a big smile. "Good morning."

Mike gave her a long look before he put the truck into reverse and backed up so he could turn around. Once they were on the road, he casually asked, "So want to tell me why you need to escape from your parents?"

She shivered and huddled deeper into her jacket. "No."

He turned up the heat. "Maybe I should ask them myself. They're pretty open. I don't think they have any secrets they're not willing to share."

Except hers. And once the truth came out—and it would—they wouldn't be able to look any of their neighbors in the eyes ever again. They'd probably have to move, and it would be all her fault.

"Please don't," she said, sorry she'd awakened his curiosity, hoping to smother it out before it got any bigger because the last thing she wanted to do was cry a waterfall in front of him. "Trust me. They don't want to talk about it and you don't want to know."

As they crested a hilltop, she peered out the window at the snow filled ditches, the thick hoar frost clinging to the trees, and the mountain range filling the landscape. Thankfully Mike didn't pursue the topic, and as the truck descended into another rolling valley, the only sound in the cab was the hum of tires against the frozen pavement, and the easy tones of a country song coming from the radio.

After a few miles, he broke the silence, his voice deep and strong and oh so casual. "You do realize that if we're going to hang out together, we're going to have to talk, right?"

Jane turned from the window and huffed out a laugh. "See, this is what I was referring to yesterday. Men and their non-stop chatter."

"Fine. Keep your secrets, Jane Watts." The hot cowboy in the driver's seat smiled a real honest to goodness smile. It lightened his eyes and vanquished the permanent pinch between his masculine brows. "What do you want to talk about instead?"

For the first time since climbing into the cab, she relaxed. "Let's discuss your plan."

"Plan?"

"Yeah. How you're going to deal with Abby." At his unfathomable look, she raised her eyebrows. "You do have a plan, don't you?"

"What's the point? Your sister hates me."

He looked so miserable, she found herself reaching out with a hand to comfort him before she caught herself. Becoming overly friendly or familiar with anyone at this point was out of the question. She clasped her hands together on her lap. "Abby hates most men, so don't take it personally."

Attention glued to the hilly, winding road, he laser focused in on that. "Why?"

She shrugged and let her gaze travel across his profile. "Near as Mom and I can figure it out, her high school boyfriend did a number on her."

Mike pulled his gaze from the road. "High school was a long time ago."

"I know. You'd think she'd be over him by now." Feeling more comfortable with him by the second, she saw how he maneuvered the truck over the snow and ice with confidence. She just couldn't see him as a loose cannon, out of control and dangerous. But then, more than anyone else, she knew she couldn't always trust her instincts. "You definitely need a plan."

"Fine." At the same time they crested the top of a hill and started down, his fingers tightened around the steering wheel and she got an uncomfortable jolt in her stomach. "All I can do is be straight with her. She knows I screwed up, so there's no point pretending I didn't. I'll go in there, apologize, and beg for custody."

"That's a bad plan."

"Do you have a better one?"

Sometimes men could be totally clueless. "You need to gain her trust."

"Trust?" He speared her with a frustrated look. "You've already said your sister doesn't trust anyone. Nothing I say will make her trust me. I have to *show* her that I can be

49

trusted."

"First off, you need to relax."

"Relax?" Now he was starting to look annoyed. "The future of my daughters is at stake here. This is as about relaxed as I'm gonna get."

She winced and shifted slightly toward the passenger door. "And most important of all, whatever she says, whatever she implies, don't show that you're mad at her."

Jaw set, gaze focused on the road, he flexed his fingers and softened his tone. "I'm not mad at Abby. I'm angry with myself for losing control like that." His expression twisted with guilt and remorse, and he released a soft laugh. "How can I gain her trust, how can I feel right about going after custody of my girls, when I don't even trust myself?"

Instinctively, Jane reached out. This time when she touched him, she didn't pull back. This time, she put her hand on his large bicep and squeezed. "You get out of bed each day with a resolve to do better, put one foot in front of the other and move forward."

And even though she felt the need to give him a hug, she didn't.

Because the man was dangerous, all right.

A danger to her heart.

He pulled up to a stop sign, applied the brakes, and the truck rolled to a stop. Automatically glancing both ways, and seeing that the coast was clear, Jane assumed he'd continue on, but when the truck continued to idle without moving, she glanced over at the man in the driver's seat. "Is something wrong?"

His expression was grim. "You tell me."

Jane frowned back at him. "What are you talking about?"

"You're hiding something, Jane Watts, and I'd like to

know what it is."

CHAPTER SIX

Jane Watts. He should have known she'd be trouble right from the moment he'd set eyes on her. Big eyes. Hollow cheeks. The same haunted look on her face that he saw when he peered into the mirror every morning.

Something bad had happened to her. Something that had turned her into this nervous, twitchy person who jumped at every shadow.

Barbara and Walter knew about it too. *That* was the change he'd noticed in them months ago. Despite being wrapped up in his own sad little world, he'd seen the new worry in their eyes, the way Barbara sometimes stepped into her husband's arms and just hung on.

And he'd known that level of sadness hadn't been about his problems, but their own.

At first, Mike had pretended to ignore the intimacy. It had hurt too much, and reminded him of the precious times he'd held Hannah in his arms. But in the months since her death, as he'd slowly climbed out of the deep, dark pit of loneliness he'd fallen into—contrary to what Barbara and everyone else thought, he didn't drink *all of the time*—he'd wondered and wanted to ask if they were okay.

And now here was their youngest daughter, staring at him with surprise and terror…and maybe if he looked close enough, squinted at just the right angle, the reluctant desire to share.

"Jane?" he prodded gently. "Anything you tell me in confidence won't leave the privacy of this truck."

"I—" She blinked, pulled her gaze from his to stare out the side window, and mumbled, "I don't want to talk about it."

Mike released the breath he'd been holding, and checking both ways, turned the truck onto the main road leading into town. "Okay, pick a topic. We can't just sit here in total silence without it bugging the hell out of me that you're pressed against that door so tightly, if the latch were to open accidentally, you'd land on your head on the asphalt."

Her head snapped around so fast, he saw her wince and rub the side of her neck. "Sorry, I just—"

Indeed, one glance at her face and he wished he could call back his hard words.

She looked so freaking sorry, he couldn't help but wonder if she'd been in an abusive relationship. It would explain the reason why she kept slipping into that timid, fearful creature that made him worry about every word he said. "Jane, topic please?"

She scrunched her forehead, as though coming up with conversation hurt. "What do you want to talk about?"

"Anything. You pick." She sucked her bottom lip into her mouth, and with her profile in his side vision, she unrolled the window slightly, rolled it back up, then repeated the movement, letting in a blast of wintery air each time. Mike gritted his teeth. "Please pick a topic you feel safe with before I freeze my balls off."

She stilled, suddenly motionless, her brow furrowed, her shoulders tensed, and he realized that she needed help far more than he did.

Did Abby know that her sister was on the verge of a full-blown meltdown? Could he discuss Jane's problem with the social worker? Even though he had his own stuff to deal with, he felt compelled to help the woman who'd stepped inside that bullpen as though she didn't care whether she lived or died.

Because he'd been there, done that, and for the sake of his girls, had to move past it.

Her soft voice interrupted his thoughts. "Here's a topic for you, if you accept my challenge. Tell me about Hannah. Your marriage. Your life together. Your children."

As if a gate had opened, memories filled his mind. He gripped the steering wheel, poleaxed by the desire to deny her request, equally eager to share everything his wife had been with someone who wouldn't look at him with just pity in her eyes. Sliding a glance her way, noting how she'd pressed against the door with trepidation, he eased back on the accelerator and forced himself to relax.

He hadn't talked about Hannah since he'd lost her.

But when he took a deep breath and released it, the words spilled out. "You grew up in the ranching community, but I was just a city boy filled with dreams of my own spread. So I worked hard, taking jobs wherever I could so I could learn the ranching business."

Easily maneuvering the truck through the crests and valleys of the road into town, he continued. "Hannah and I married young. She supported my dream to buy the ranch, but it wasn't easy for her. Fortunately Barbara and Walter were there to answer our questions and guide us whenever we needed help."

Out the corner of his eye, he saw the tenseness in her body start to ease. He hunched over the steering wheel and continued. "Even though we were blessed with a beautiful life filled with love and laughter and a future filled with possibilities, we had problems too. One failed pregnancy, then a second one, and then a third."

His voice drifted off as he remembered how much Hannah had wanted a family and how heartbroken she'd been with each miscarriage.

"Maybe the universe had been attempting to tell me something, but I didn't pay attention. After all, it wasn't me that wanted a family. I'd already gotten what I wanted. Hannah and the ranch." He sighed. "But Hannah wanted children so badly, and I wanted her to be happy, so we kept trying."

He glanced at the silent woman now watching him with an intentness that made him embarrassed for revealing the truth. He shifted on the seat. "It's how I got into bull riding. Even though I started late, I was good at it and since I wanted to pay off the ranch as quickly as possible, I joined the rodeo circuit."

Jane's soft voice interrupted him. "And that's when Hannah became pregnant with the twins?"

He nodded, glum. "Pregnant and taking care of the ranch every weekend while I went from town to town trying to win enough prize money to support us. I barely made it home for the birth of the twins."

"And then you fell in love with your daughters." There was hope in her voice and something more...certainty.

Mike was about to disappoint her. "Not at first. I wanted boys to carry on the family name and the ranch. I knew nothing about babies or little girls, and so the care for them fell to Hannah while I continued to rack up prize wins wherever I went." He gave a harsh laugh. "I knew nothing about being a father. Everything I'd learned from my dad was not appropriate for the life I wanted for my family."

He fell silent, took a deep breath to steady himself, and inhaled the scent of his passenger's soap. It tickled his nose and awakened his senses and made him aware of her as an attractive woman.

He glanced at her profile—thankfully she was engrossed in the passing scenery—then turned back to the road.

She had one of those faces a man could get lost in. Not a model perfect face, but she had strong bones, a ready smile, and laugh lines around her mouth and eyes. And those eyes....she'd looked at him and he'd been instantly—stupidly—mesmerized by the color of her eyes.

The noise of the heater and the radio playing softly filled the silent cab and gave him time to think about how much he missed his girls, and he knew he'd do anything to get them back.

He'd been a fool to fall apart like that. A fool to allow his emotions to rule his head.

He took a breath and forced himself to continue. "Then Hannah fell ill and nothing existed in my world, but my wife and girls. I've never told anyone this before. I don't know if Hannah discussed it with Harley, but if she did, Harley never said a word to me. Never blamed me either."

He swiped at the moisture in his eyes and had to clear his throat before he spoke again. "There you have it. The whole ugly story."

"It's not so ugly." She faced him, her expression solemn, concerned, and wary. "Abby can be really stubborn."

Mike pulled himself out of the past and back to the present. He'd dealt with Jane's sister months ago, and the sooner he was done with her and this whole mess he'd created, the better he'd like it. "Tell me about it. I'm pretty sure begging won't help, but what other option do I have?"

"I could come in with you."

The tone of her voice suggested she wanted to do anything *but* that. Still, he was almost desperate enough to take advantage of her offer. "She'd see that we're friends and maybe she'd soften her attitude."

"Something like that."

Almost, he thought to himself as he remembered that she had her own problems, and whatever they were, they were potentially bigger than his own screw up. "If you come in with me, Abby will tell you not to get involved with me."

"I'm...not involved." She smiled across the cab at him, appearing more relaxed than before he'd told her his sad tale. "It's just one friend supporting another."

Mike forced a grin and tried to relax, but it was impossible, not with the thought of the social worker's judgment sitting on his shoulders. "Ah, so now we're moving on to the friend part of our relationship."

Jane huffed out a laugh. "Focusing on your problems helps me forget about mine."

He turned on his signal light, steered the truck left, and drove into town, reminded that she needed help as much as he did...perhaps more. As they reached their destination and he angle parked, the freshly fallen snow crunching beneath the tires, he moved to turn off the truck, then stopped. "Jane, what I said earlier. I meant it."

She grabbed the door handle and he heard the latch click open.

"I know," she said softly without looking at him. "But trust me, you do not want to hear *my* story."

Then she pushed open the truck door, jumped outside, and slammed the door shut.

Mike turned the key in the ignition and the motor stopped. As he watched her stuff her hands into the pockets of her jacket and step up onto the curb, he knew that she was wrong.

He climbed out of the truck, wishing he could pin her down and ease her pain. But right now, he needed to focus on what was right in front of him. Abby and her decision.

He contemplated a future without his girls and knew that if he didn't pull this off, he'd never be able to face them again. He'd watch from afar as Gage and Harley adopted the twins and raised them as their own. He'd be hidden on the sidelines as they graduated, got married, and had babies of their own. He'd grow old alone and lonely, dreading the day when he had to face Hannah and be judged for his actions.

As he joined Jane outside the office, her expression was soft and compassionate. "You're right. It's best if you meet with Abby alone. I'll sit in the waiting room. Just remember that I'm cheering you on."

Instinctively, he reached out and brushed a strand of hair off the side of her face and tucked it behind her ear. When she flinched, he immediately withdrew and stepped back, and he wondered again if there was an abusive ex out there. And if the bastard was looking for her right this very moment. "Thanks. I owe you big time for your support."

"I'm sure it will all work out in your favor. Abby's not a monster." She flinched at the last word, then seemed to catch herself as she squared her shoulders and gave him a strained smile. "It'll be fine. Just keep that big old country boy smile on your face and maybe it'll charm her."

"I don't think there's a man on this planet who could charm your sister," he muttered as he held the office door open for her, then followed her in, went to the front desk, and spoke to the receptionist. "I'm here to see Abby."

The receptionist nodded. "Please, have a seat. She'll be with you shortly."

While she picked up the phone to announce him, Mike unzipped his jacket and took the seat next to Jane.

He was nervous. Sweating nervous. Beside him, Jane had picked up a magazine, looking through it casual as could be, but he could sense her agitation as though it were his own. Plus, she was holding it upside down.

What did she have to lose? If Abby said no, Jane would return to her life...and Mike would be crushed.

Down the hallway, a door swung open and the social worker stepped out. As she walked toward them, Mike pushed to his feet, taking in her almost belligerent attitude, and the self-serving satisfaction of a woman with an axe to grind.

There were similarities between the two sisters—the long, blonde hair, the mauve color of their irises. But Abby always had her hair swept into a tight knot on the top of her head and her body shouted confidence and arrogance. She was about two inches shorter than Jane, which was about the same height as Hannah.

Her hard gaze slid from him to her sister and instantly softened, and as she stepped into the reception area, her trajectory veered off in that direction. She greeted Jane with an apprehensive hug, almost as though she expected to be rejected. "Nice to see you out of that bedroom."

Jane's cheeks flushed as she pulled out of the hug and wrinkled her nose. "It's nice to be out of that bedroom."

Abby opened her mouth to say something more, then seemed to change her mind. Only then did she turn her judging stare on Mike.

He held out his hand. "Thanks for seeing me on such short notice."

Almost reluctantly, she took his hand and shook it briefly, her own hand icy cold, then withdrew it quickly. "I'd prefer to see you alone."

He nodded, knowing that the social worker wouldn't like him hanging out with her sister. "That's the plan. Jane's just here because she's bored."

Abby turned briefly to Jane, her gaze steady on her sister's face, her expression serious. "I want to talk to you afterwards, so don't run away."

At Jane's nod, Abby turned and strode down the hallway. Mike followed her, but before he stepped into her office, he glanced back down the hallway toward the reception area and met Jane's anxious gaze. Despite the worried frown puckering her brow, she gave him a hopeful smile and a two-thumbs-up.

Mike pulled his gaze away, stepped inside the lion's den, and closed the door behind him.

Abby gestured toward a chair. "Have a seat."

"Thank you."

He waited for her to sit down before he did, and as he dropped onto the chair, he saw her grab a file folder from the tray on her orderly desk, set it down in front of her, then fold her hands on top as she eyed him with suspicion.

"How have you been, Mike?"

She sounded like a damn psychologist.

"Good," he lied and forced himself not to squirm.

"Your message said that you want to regain custody of the girls."

"That's correct."

She stared at him and he stared back, wondering if this were a test or a competition, wondering whether he'd come out the winner or loser. Ever since she'd discovered Hannah's condition in the late stages of her breast cancer, Abby had had it in for him, almost as if she blamed him. The two women had been best friends, so maybe she did.

Her mouth turned down at the corners. Then she gave a put upon sigh, flipped open the folder, and without even looking at it, said, "Request denied."

He jerked forward which caused her to raise one eyebrow, and he froze mid-jerk, forcing himself to remain calm and cool headed. "You can't do that, Abby. They're *my* daughters."

She sat forward and flipped through the pages in the file. "You're a danger to the girls. It's all here in black and white."

"I—" He sat back, wiped one hand across his mouth, and wished he had a drink, then immediately deleted the thought for fear it would show up on his face. One look at Abby's sour expression told him it was too late. He ground his molars together. "I would never hurt them and you know it."

Glancing at his file, she said, "You quit your therapy. According to your neighbors, you're drunk all of the time."

"I've stopped drinking."

She sat back and appeared to relax into the chair, the judgmental expression daring him to lie. "For how long?"

Okay, so she had him there. He shifted his feet under his chair, guilty. "Since last night. But I swear, I'm never touching it again."

"And the bull riding? The girls have lost one parent. I'm not going to put them through losing another." Before he could answer, she closed the file, glanced at her watch, and stood up, indicating that they were done. "If you'll excuse me, I have another appointment."

Mike pushed to his feet, uncertain what to do. All he knew was that he couldn't leave without some kind of hope. Otherwise, he might as well go back to the way things were before Nate told him about the adoption. He kept his voice low, even. "Abby, work with me here. Tell me what I have to do." His voice grew thick and despite the sudden moisture in his eyes, forced himself to continue. "I love my girls and you know it."

The hard look on her face relaxed slightly, and for just a split second, he could see pity in her gaze. But even then, she could barely look him in the eye. She moved around the desk toward the door. "Well, for starters you can get back into therapy."

"Done," he said without hesitation. "What about visitation rights?"

The hard look was back in her eyes. "I'll discuss it with the twins and Gage and Harley, and let you know."

Mike realized he wasn't going to get any further. Not today. He moved toward the door where he stopped and held out his hand. "Thank you for your time."

She ignored his hand and her eyes narrowed on his face. "Why are you with my sister?"

Mike blinked and lowered his hand. He'd sort of forgotten that Jane was out in the reception area waiting for him. "I'm not *with* her, if that's what you're insinuating. She's bored and offered her support. Frankly, I could use someone's support."

Her lips curled into a sneer, and she leaned toward him and jabbed one sharp fingernail into his chest. "If you hurt her, if you so much as raise your voice to her, I will make sure you never see your girls again. She's already been through enough. She doesn't need you complicating her life. Understand?"

He understood perfectly well. It made him realize that he shouldn't be dragging Jane into his messy life. He'd screwed up alone. He should fix this alone. Except that dealing with everything alone during Hannah's illness had been a big part of the reason he'd gone over the edge in the first place.

Acknowledging that he understood, he nodded, then got out of there as quickly as possible. When Jane saw him coming down the hallway, she pushed to her feet, her expression bright with hope. "How did it go?"

He didn't want to talk about it here, not with Abby able to hear his every word. "I'll wait outside while you talk with your sister."

But when he headed out into the crisp morning air, Jane followed him.

"Mike, what happened?"

He faced her and found himself falling into the clear depths of her mauve gaze. Abby was right. He couldn't be trusted, and the last thing he wanted to do was drag this woman into his problems and hurt her. "Jane, I can do this on my own."

In a heartbeat, the woman in front of him shed her timidness. Teeth gritted, hands fisted at her sides, she repeated her question. "What happened?"

He shrugged and moved closer to the lioness in front of him to allow more room for an elderly gentleman to shuffle past. "Your sister doesn't like me very much."

"My sister has always had bad taste in men." She continued to stare up at him, judging his silence and narrowing her eyes at him. "What did she threaten you with?"

He lowered his voice so the people walking past them couldn't hear. "Therapy."

"That's no biggie. It'll do you good."

He pinned her with a serious look. "And she doesn't like the fact that we're hanging out together."

And even though she kept her gaze fixed on his face, he saw the protective shield drop down into place. "Abby is just being overprotective."

"Why?"

She sidestepped toward the office door. "I better go talk to her."

"Whatever you do, don't mention my name or you'll make her problems with me worse."

"No, I won't, I promise."

Mike watched her turn, sprint away, and disappear into the building.

His heart climbed into his throat because he knew her fierceness was all in his defense.

CHAPTER SEVEN

Jane stepped into her sister's office, closed the door behind her, and leaned back against it. "What was that all about?"

Abby sat behind her desk and didn't bother looking up from the file in front of her. "What took you so long?"

"Ha ha." She plunked down on one of the chairs and attempted to relax but inside, her stomach felt tight and uncomfortable. "Okay, spill. What's going on between you and Mike?"

"Nothing," Abby mumbled while she made a notation on one of the papers.

"You turned down his request."

"Of course I did." She set aside the pen in her hand, raised her gaze, and leaned back on the chair. "Why are you involved in Mike's affairs?"

Trying to appear nonchalant, she shrugged. "Because I have nothing better to do and I was getting claustrophobic at home."

Abby sat forward, her elbows on the top of the desk, her hands clasped together in front of her. "I'm going to give you the same recommendation I gave Mike. You need to get into therapy. You're bottling things up, attempting to pretend they didn't happen. But you need to deal with it, Jane. You need to let someone in to help you."

The tightness in her stomach grew almost painful, and spread to her chest and arms. She fought against the sudden urge to curl up into a ball and hide her shame. Not even her sister knew the extent of what she'd been through. She kept her tone calm and easy. "I'm not here about me, Abby. I'm here to help Mike. He deserves a second chance." When her sister didn't reply, she asked, "What do you want from him?"

"I want him to take responsibility."

She frowned, confused. "Isn't that what he's trying to do?"

"No." There was something different in her sister's expression. Something Jane couldn't quite put her finger on. "Mike wasn't there when Hannah needed him. He wasn't there for his daughters. He took the easy way out, Jane."

Exasperation wiped the shame away and she pushed to her feet, ready to fight for the man who's lost everything including the woman he loved. "Cut him some slack. He'd just lost his wife."

Abby snorted and stood. "That's just an excuse."

There was so much hate on her sister's face, Jane took a step back and bumped into the seat of the chair. "Wow, when did you become so hard and unmovable?"

Her own frustration showing, Abby raked her fingers through her hair. "This isn't an easy job, Jane. I have to weed through the lies and the bullshit. I have to see past the phoniness and the posturing. My chief concern is always the kids. Is that wrong?"

"No, of course not. That's how it should be."

A TIME TO BE TENDER

Her sister's fierce expression softened as she came around the desk and stopped in front of her. "Did he tell you what he did?"

Jane met her sister's gaze. "No. And I didn't ask."

Abby's tone was flat and angry. "After Hannah died, Mike started drinking heavily. His sister-in-law finally had to help him with the twins. When things started to fall apart at home, he abused the girls, threatened his sister-in-law, then rather than sober up and shoulder the consequences, he ran away."

For just a moment, she saw the nightmare in her sister's story. But then she remembered how gentle Mike had been when he'd asked her about *her* story. Jane couldn't reconcile the man she was getting to know with the man her sister spoke of. "You're wrong about him, Abby."

"Am I? Later, he broke into his brother's house and held everyone at knifepoint. If not for Gage's interference, Mike would be sitting in a jail cell instead of wandering about freely." Abby softened her voice. "Jane, monsters appear wearing the friendliest of faces. You of all people should know that. Stay away from that man. I can't protect you if you ignore my advice."

Anger infused her so suddenly, she just barely managed to stop herself from lashing out. She took a step back. "Protect me? Where were you that night? I wouldn't have even been there if you hadn't blown me off to take off with some guy you didn't even know."

Abby's expression contorted with guilt before she covered her face with her hands and whispered, "I know and I'm so sorry."

In an instant, Jane's anger deflated. She loved her sister and didn't want to ruin their relationship. "Forget I said anything."

Abby whispered back, "You know I won't."

Jane sighed. "Look, maybe I just need some space right now. Time to get my head on straight and figure out what I'm going to do with the rest of my life."

Abby jerked her head up, clearly surprised. "Aren't you going back to teaching?"

Turning her back on her sister, she grabbed the door handle and pulled open the door. There was so much pain in her heart and in her chest. "Probably not. They won't want me back when the truth comes out."

Then she walked out before her sister could say another word and ruin what little peace she'd found in the past few months. But when she stepped out into the chilly morning air, she immediately saw Mike. He was leaning against the front bumper of the truck, dark sunglasses hiding his eyes, his expression impassive, and when he saw her, he straightened and opened the door for her, all gentlemanly and old fashioned.

As she climbed into the truck, she wished she could see below the surface package—past the angular cut of his jaw, the broad shoulders and killer abs, the cowboy cockiness that was born into a select breed of men—to the center of his being.

To his heart.

The edge of his mouth turned up into a self-deprecative grin. "When you stare at me like that, it looks like you're trying to see the monster inside of me."

Was she an idiot for wanting to trust him? Her parents liked him, but that didn't mean squat. He really could be a monster, and this time...this time...

She might not survive.

"I'd like to go home now," she said suddenly. She reached for the door handle and pulled the door shut, forcing Mike out of the way of the closing door. As he walked around the front of the truck and climbed inside, Jane pulled out her phone and texted her mom that Mike would be dropping her off at home in the next half hour or so. That way if he took her back to his place and...

His deep voice interrupted her, and she jumped and hit her head against the passenger door window.

"What did you say?" she asked as she scowled across at him and rubbed the side of her head.

"I asked if you were okay. You seem kind of jumpy and nervous all of a sudden."

Jane noticed that she was squashed into the corner of the truck, smashed against the passenger door as though she could make herself invisible.

"I'm not afraid of you," she said, but her voice didn't sound convincing, so she sat up straight and repeated herself, enunciating each word with hopes of convincing him...and herself. "I...am...not...afraid...of...you."

Exasperation flashed across his handsome features. "Hell, that's great, because you're terrifying the bejesus out of me."

She frowned, caught off guard and suspicious. And when she didn't say anything further, he started the truck, backed out of the parking spot, and drove down the road. When he finally broke the silence, his voice was too casual, too easy.

"Would you like to know what I've decided to do?"

Oh no, here it came. The fool-me-once, fool-me-twice scenario. Maybe she deserved whatever came her way. She could practically see the judge and jury's incredulous expressions as they listened to her testify—

Yes, I know, how stupid of me to trust another stranger.

Mike's voice interrupted her thoughts again. "I'm going

to prove Abby wrong. I'm going to go back to the ranch and clean up the house and get it ready for the girls. Then I'm going to call your sister's office every freaking day until she gives in and gives me a chance to prove myself."

As a wave of guilt washed over her, Jane sat up straight. Here she'd been thinking all kinds of terrible things, but the man was just planning his strategy to get his daughters back. "That's great."

He glanced her way, then back at the road. "I'd ask you to help, you know, to give you an excuse to get out of your parents' house, but I totally understand your predicament. It's clear you're uncomfortable when you're alone with me."

Jane put one hand to her mouth, chewed on her thumbnail, and tried to deny his accusation. "No, I'm not—"

"Yes, you are," he interrupted. "No worries though, Jane. I took care of Hannah and the twins and the house and the ranch for the last few months of my wife's illness without anyone to help me. I can do it now too."

He fell silent at that point. Silent and contemplative and focused on the road ahead.

Jane felt as though she were barely breathing, her gaze straight ahead, waiting for that moment when he veered off the road to take her elsewhere. It wasn't until he'd turned the truck into the lane leading to her parents' house that she finally felt the tight band around her chest begin to loosen.

As the truck rolled to a stop in the driveway and Jane grabbed the door handle to escape, his voice halted her departure.

"If I don't see you again, Jane, I hope you have a nice life. You deserve it."

"Thanks. You too," she mumbled, already half out of

the truck. When her feet hit the ground and she turned to shut the truck door, she recognized the kindness in his eyes, the understanding too.

He smiled and put the truck into reverse. "And if you change your mind or decide you want to talk, text me. You're more than welcome to hang with me until you're ready to face the rest of the world again."

Jane watched him drive away, and with a sickening feeling in her stomach, realized that if she didn't find the courage to take him up on his offer, she might be here hiding at her parents' house for the rest of her life.

CHAPTER EIGHT

By the time Mike returned to the ranch, he dreaded the thought of entering the house where it had all ended so badly. And when he stepped into the kitchen and faced the mess he'd left behind, he froze, gut churning, ears roaring.

All around him were the ravages of his life, and in every inch of the room were memories of the woman he'd once loved and the life he'd destroyed.

He hadn't been inside since he'd gone ballistic. The thought of it now—sober and clearheaded—made him feel ashamed and regretful. No wonder Abby refused to trust him with the twins.

He'd stepped over the line, so far over he couldn't see it in the distance anymore. There was absolutely no excuse for his actions, but he'd learned his lesson. Booze and him didn't mix. One drink led to another, which ultimately led to him losing control.

It was all on his shoulders, and he knew exactly what Hannah would say if she was up there looking down right now.

Oh Mike, how could I have trusted you with our babies?

Shame and guilt overwhelmed him, and he almost turned and hightailed it back outside.

But that wouldn't win over Abby or the twins.

Mike forced his legs to carry him through the kitchen and down the hallway where he tapped the lever of the thermostat to nudge up the heat. He heard the furnace click in, and a few seconds later he could feel heat coming out of the floor registers. As he reentered the kitchen, he stopped to survey the mess.

Beer cans littered the floor, and those that weren't scattered about were stacked into a triangular pile at one end of the long wooden table his wife had lovingly selected for their growing family. Despite the stuffy, stale air surrounding him, he swore he could still smell the sweet scent of Hannah's perfume.

He closed his mind to the memory and noticed that along with the mess, a fine layer of dust coated everything. Moving from room to room, he opened the windows to air out the unused house.

Soon, the winter freshness of the outside air drifted through the rooms, and he forced himself to concentrate. He tossed the empties into a large green garbage bag, collected dirty dishes from around the house, and when the temperature in the house grew too cool for even him, he retraced his steps from room to room and closed the windows.

As the roar in his ears subsided, other sounds made their way into his brain. The creak of the house as it shifted in the frozen ground of the prairie winter. Air blowing from the registers to replace the coolness in the house with warmth. Memories of the twins' giggles and Hannah's laughter.

He stopped in the middle of the family room, his eyes

hot with unshed tears, and took in the toys scattered on the hardwood floor, the picture frames along the fireplace mantel that he'd turned facedown during a drunken outburst.

Once upon a time, his family had been incredibly and crazily happy.

Once upon a time, his life had been perfect.

Mike picked up a picture, blew the dust off the frame, and stood it back up. It was a photo of Hannah sitting in the rocker with the newborn twins in her arms, a gentle smile turning up the edges of her mouth, love shining in her eyes as she gazed up at the camera...at him.

His heart cracked, and he rubbed at the center of his chest and took a deep breath in an effort to contain the pain of his loss.

Once, the house had been filled with his wife's gentle care and continuous laughter. And when the twins arrived, first Laura, then a few minutes later, Lisa, their home had been filled with love and laughter and a happiness that had survived night feedings, lack of sleep, and every challenge that a new parent could experience.

Hannah had handled it all with grace and good cheer. She'd loved being a wife and mother, and as he headed toward the kitchen, he remembered her making chocolate chip cookies with the twins, could almost smell the rich gooey buttery flavor of her favorite recipe.

Grabbing the garbage bag full of beer cans, he tied the bag shut and carried it to the back door where he tossed it outside onto the porch. Then he returned to the kitchen, gathered up the dirty tea towels, and carried them to the main floor laundry room. The sight there stopped him cold.

Piles of dirty clothes were scattered on the floor, and he vaguely remembered the moment when the last of his life had fallen apart. He'd tried to drown his grief in a bottle of whiskey, then chased out the twins because even in his drunken state, he'd had enough common sense to know that they didn't need to witness their daddy falling apart.

And then he'd cornered his sister-in-law in the laundry room. After days of being cooped up with the one woman in the world who looked *exactly* like his wife, he'd been a raving lunatic. He'd threatened her and tried to kiss her. Thank goodness his brother had shown up before things had gotten too far out of hand.

For the last few months, Gage had continued to check on him, but his sister-in-law had stayed away from him. Far, far away, and he couldn't blame her. Maybe it was time to mend their broken relationship.

Mike pressed his palm against his chest, the pressure inside overwhelming.

It was better not to feel anything, better to keep a shield around his tender heart and not let anyone get too close.

His cell phone buzzed and he pulled it out of his shirt pocket to see a text from Jane. After the way they'd parted—the haunted look in her mauve eyes, the near-terror expression on her face—he hadn't expected to hear from her again.

What are you doing?

He thumbed a reply. *Cleaning up the house.*

A minute or more went past before her reply came through. *So I'll ride Pepper over, and when you get sick of me and my help, you can kick me out.*

The woman was trying to hide from something, and he found himself wondering if his problems were minuscule in comparison to hers.

And then his thumbs were moving across the tiny keyboard before he could consider the fact that letting her deeper into his world would no doubt complicate his life even more. *Make sure you dress for the weather. There's a cold front moving in this afternoon.*

CHAPTER NINE

For the next week, Mike worked alongside Jane, feeling much like an intruder in his own home. He was thankful for her help, but more than that, he was thankful for her company. It made the long days in the quiet, empty house not quite so quiet or empty.

Day by day, room by room, they vacuumed and dusted and washed until the house was spotless, and he was satisfied it would pass Abby's inspection. And by late afternoon, Jane always rode off to return to the Watts ranch before the sun set and the temperature dropped too much for the cold, dark winter night.

Left alone, Mike avoided the house and the memories. Memories that still robbed him of air and made him wish he could drown his sorrow in the bottom of a bottle of whiskey.

The worst of it all was the loneliness. Without the booze, there was nothing to deaden his senses and he felt every lonely moment like a stake to the heart.

Instead, he busied himself with interior repairs to the barn and the stables, and by the time he went to bed each night, he fell into an exhausted sleep muddled with dreams of Hannah and the twins...and Jane.

This morning, he'd chosen to clear the driveway and drive pad after a night of snow, just to escape the house and Jane's presence. He found himself watching her, noticing the way she moved, brisk and efficient. The way she stretched out the kinks in her back, raising her arms above her head, arching her back like a cat.

The movement drew his attention to the way the soft material of her sweater hugged her full breasts. To the narrowness of her ribcage and waist. To the soft curve of her hips and roundness of her derrière.

And he couldn't help but wonder what she was doing here.

With him.

What had happened that had brought shadows into her eyes and a sad tilt to her mouth? Even though he swore he didn't want to know, as each day moved into the next, he found himself dwelling on the mystery of her more and more.

The more he dwelled on thoughts of Jane, the further he felt from the woman he'd once loved so much.

It had been barely six months since Hannah died. Yet in many ways, he felt as though his wife had been gone much longer. She'd been sick for so long, they'd become more caregiver and patient than husband and wife.

And the guilt always riding his shoulders increased.

It had been bad enough feeling guilty that he couldn't do anything to save Hannah or take care of their girls, but he never expected to find himself attracted to another woman.

He glanced up at the house, and the memory of his wife enfolded him. He could still see her sitting in the late spring sunshine on the porch, a scarf covering her head to hide her baldness from the radiation treatments, her favorite blanket wrapped around her shoulders to ward off the chill.

Even then, when she'd stood so near to death's door, she'd find a smile for him and the girls. She'd been happy and beautiful and his for a short time. There'd always been something so out-of-this-world about her. Maybe it was because she'd been destined to only be on this planet for a short time.

And he'd been the lucky bastard to have her in his life, even if it had only been for a little while.

Now he found himself watching Jane, hungering for the feel of her lips under his, the press of her body against his. But they were friends, nothing more. There was no room in his life for the *more*, not when his focus needed to be on getting custody of the twins.

He stopped to lean on the edge of the shovel and glanced up at the sunny sky. "Well, Hannah, what do you have to say?"

But instead of his wife's cryptic reply, he heard a vehicle drive into the yard. As he wiped the moisture from his eyes, he recognized Sara Coltrane's Jeep. It turned into the driveway and pulled into the spot beside his truck. Mike headed her way as the driver's door swung open. "Hey, Sara. You're parked a little tight to my truck, don't you think?"

"No, it's okay, there's plenty of room." She swung one leg out, planted her foot on the snow packed driveway, and tried to slide out, but her very pregnant belly wouldn't fit through the opening. She looked up at him, her eyes narrowed. "Don't you dare say a word. Don't you dare laugh at me either."

Mike felt the edges of his mouth twitch up. "In a few

years, you'll look back on this moment and see the humor in it."

"Not likely." She settled back behind the steering wheel and reached for the door handle. "Move back so I don't accidentally run over your big feet."

This time, as the vehicle door slammed shut, Mike let the smile out and watched as Sara maneuvered the Jeep on the driveway, leaving enough room between the Jeep and his truck for a full grown elephant to walk through.

He was thankful for her presence. Sara was the only person who still treated him as though he hadn't screwed up his entire life. Maybe because she felt as though she'd totally screwed up her own.

As soon as the vehicle stopped, he opened the door wide and offered his hand. "Here, let me help you. I *think* you might have enough room to maneuver now."

She took his hand, and when she finally gained her feet, she was tall and lanky and looked like she had an oversized basketball stuffed under the front of her jacket. Jane was going to love her.

He returned her hug, then patted her belly. "How's the kid?"

"Busy. I don't know what she's doing in there. Either baking cakes or roping steers. Whatever it is, she's awake all night." She gave him a doleful look. "Which means I'm awake all night too."

"She's getting you ready for those nighttime feedings." He took her by the elbow and turned her toward the house. "Come on. Let's get out of the cold and take a load off your feet."

"It's so not fair," she grumbled as he steadied her across the snow and ice. "Hale had all the fun, freaked out like a little girl, then ran away. And I get stuck fat and ugly."

He smirked. "You're not ugly."

She stopped and narrowed her eyes at him. "So you're saying I'm fat?"

This time he laughed out loud, and some of the pressure in his chest eased. "No. You're beautiful. Pregnant and beautiful. Hale was an idiot for running away."

"Amen to that." With a grimace, she set one hand at the small of her back and did an awkward stretch. "Dad asked me to check up on you."

Mike quirked one brow. "He did?"

"Yeah, he's pretty worried you're going over the edge." She peered up into his face, concern in her dark brown eyes. "You're not, are you? I wonder for purely selfish reasons, you know. Since my parents have no siblings and neither do I, my baby needs all the uncles and aunts she can get."

With a certainty he hadn't felt in months, he replied. "I'm not going anywhere, Sara, I promise."

"Good," she said.

He held the screen door open and motioned her inside. "In you go. Careful though, I'm not sure that the opening is big enough for you and your oversized basketball."

"Ha ha," she snorted as she stepped inside, grimaced again, and rubbed her lower back. "How did Hannah ever manage twins? She was half my size."

He really liked Sara. Besides being his best friend's daughter, she was sort of a screw up like him. "Hannah loved being pregnant, even when her feet swelled to twice their size."

"Great. Something else to look forward to," she grumbled.

As Jane entered the porch, her eyes meeting his, he

couldn't deny that there was something there, something that started a buzz low in his body and made him wish she'd come into his life when he'd finally gotten it back together.

She turned her attention to their visitor and smiled. "Sara? Little Sara Coltrane? Oh my goodness, you're all grown up."

With a ready smile, Sara held out her arm and shook Jane's hand. "Yep, it's me, in the flesh. Nice to see you again, Jane. I heard you were visiting your parents."

A worried frown creased Jane's brow as she eyed the younger woman. "What's wrong, honey?"

"I've got the backache of all backaches today." Sara rubbed at her back and grimaced. "Don't worry. It's nothing. I must have just slept funny last night."

As Mike helped Sara remove her coat, he frowned. "Maybe I should take you in to see George."

"In case you haven't heard the local gossip, I'm pregnant *and* unmarried," Sara said to Jane as she ignored him and toed off her boots, then bent down awkwardly to set the boots to the side. She straightened and rubbed at her hip.

He'd noticed that she'd been walking funny. "What's wrong with your hip?"

"Along with the backache, I have a pinch in my hip too. *Yay, fun times.* I'm actually headed into town to see the chiropractor, so besides checking on you, I thought I'd see if you wanted me to pickup anything."

"No, we're good." Mike frowned. "I'll come into town with you."

"I'm fine, really." She rubbed her back. "Although this nagging pain is getting pretty annoying. Good thing I'm going to the chiropractor."

Jane took her arm. "Come on, honey, let's get you seated somewhere comfortable."

Over Sara's head, Mike exchanged a look with Jane. "When's your due date?"

"Not for another month." She rubbed her back again and peered at Mike. "I am never ever doing this again. How other women go through it—"

Her voice drifted away, and Mike recalled bringing his own babies home from the hospital, bundled up and screaming in their car seats in the backseat while Hannah sat between them. And for the entire trip home, they'd both tried not to panic at the realization of the responsibility of the two precious bundles now in their care.

"The first time you hold your baby in your arms, you'll forget all about the pain." He cleared his thoughts and refocused on her. "Maybe you should stay here till your parents return home."

"Thanks, but I'm okay." She rubbed her back again and groaned. "Besides, I have Sam and I wouldn't want to leave him—"

A gush of liquid came from between her legs.

Mike stared at the puddle on the floor, aware of Jane and Sara doing exactly the same.

"I—I—" Confusion lit the younger woman's face and she made a move toward the kitchen. "I'm so sorry. I'll clean this up."

"No, Sara." Jane's voice softened. "Your water just broke. Looks like you're going to have this baby a wee bit early. I have some sweats you can change into and then we're taking you to the hospital."

Sara squeaked. "Early? But my mom? My dad?"

Jane took Sara's elbow. "First babies take a really long time, honey, so they have plenty of time to get home."

Mike grabbed his truck keys. "Your job is to stay calm and breathe through the pain. Let Jane and I handle the details." Then he pulled his phone out of his jacket pocket and punched speed dial. As he headed out to start the truck, the other end picked up. "George, Sara's water broke. We'll meet you at the hospital in thirty minutes."

By the time he had the truck started and warmed up, Jane had Sara changed and ready to go.

"I don't understand," the younger woman said, confusion and fear mingling on her expression as she climbed awkwardly into the back seat, Jane right behind her. "It's too early. It's a whole month early."

Mike put the truck into gear and headed down the driveway. "He must be in a rush to get started."

"She. It's a girl." She hiccuped and her voice wobbled. "My parents—"

Mike glanced in the rearview mirror. "I've already called them. They're heading to the airport now."

Her worried gaze settled on his face. "Will they make it in time?"

Mike watched Jane take Sara's hand. "I'm sure they'll try as hard as they can. But we're here for you, Sara, and we're not leaving you to go through this alone."

He heard Sara's muffled sound of pain and Jane's, "Hurry, Mike."

By the time they reached the hospital, Sara's contractions were only minutes apart. Mike dropped the women off at the front door, then parked the truck and stared at the hospital entrance. The last thing he wanted to do was go inside. There were too many bad memories of Hannah's illness, yet he couldn't just walk out on Sara. Nate would have his head.

Shoring up his manhood, he headed inside. By the time

he found the women, they were putting Sara into a wheelchair. She immediately grabbed his hand. "Mike, please don't leave me. If Mom and Dad don't make it, I want you with me."

He frowned. "Sara, I can't stay with you. I'm not your husband."

"My mom was supposed to be here. I can't do this alone."

He looked at Jane for support. "Maybe Jane could—"

Sara gripped his hand tighter and addressed Jane. "No offense, but I don't know you well enough to show you my—uh—you know."

Jane grinned. "No offense taken."

Mike could feel his throat get tighter. "And yet you're willing to show me your—uh—"

Sara nodded. "We're more like brother and sister. It's not like we're ever going to date, right?"

As the younger woman bent into another contraction, Mike caved. He glanced back at Jane. "The second Jessie gets here, she better come rescue me. Can you please call Harley and Gage, and let them know too?"

And then they were being wheeled down the hallway.

Mike glanced back once, saw Jane on her cell, then focused entirely on Sara. Her dark gaze was desperate and afraid. "Don't worry. Everything will be fine."

Once Sara was settled and comfortable in a room, her bottom lip protruded, reminding Mike of his own daughters in the middle of a sulk.

She said, "I want my mom."

And he replied, "I want your mom too."

Which thankfully made her smile.

A nurse came in. "Are you the father of the baby?"

Sara snorted. "This baby doesn't have a father."

Mike exchanged a look with the nurse and shook his head. "No, I'm a close family friend. Her parents are out of town, so I've been arm twisted into babysitting duty."

Sara snorted again. "You'll babysit all right. In fact, every time I go out, I'm calling you to babysit my kid."

He laughed. "I'll have to arm wrestle your mom and dad for babysitting rights. I've seen your mom wrestle down your dad. She's scary strong."

Another contraction gripped her, and Mike let her squeeze his hand until he thought she might break his fingers. As the pain eased, she released his hand and flushed. "Sorry. I hope I didn't hurt you."

He brushed some hair off her sweaty face, then rested his forearms on the edge of the bed. "I'm here, Sara, and I'm not going anywhere."

Tears of gratitude filled her gaze and leaked out of the corner of her eyes. But before she could say anything, the door swung open and Dr. George Davis strode into the room. He stopped when he saw Mike.

"Well, I'll be damned. I didn't expect to see you here."

"Yeah, yeah," Mike muttered, suddenly self-conscious. "Don't say a word. Today is all about Sara."

George smiled and turned his attention to the young woman. "So how are you doing, kid?"

Sara gasped as another contraction gripped her belly and she grabbed Mike's hand. There was a desperate look in her eyes. "George, Emma's not due for another month—"

His expression softened, and he gently squeezed her calf. "Don't you worry, Sara. Everything looked great during your last exam. Your little one is just eager to meet you."

George turned efficient and prepared to examine the

patient.

Mike was suddenly glad he hadn't left Sara alone. Besides, if he did, Nate would have had him by the balls and Jessie would never have spoken to him again. He'd been through this with the twins. He had experience and Sara was still just a kid, probably more terrified than she let on.

As another contraction gripped her, she ground out, "Thank you. Both of you. Thank you so much."

Sitting here brought back memories of the birth of his girls. He'd stayed with Hannah every moment. He'd rubbed her back and fed her ice chips to keep her hydrated through the birth. Maybe he could ease some of Sara's pain.

As the contraction ended and time passed by in a blur of pain and boredom, and George came in and out, Mike tried to rub her back and feed her ice cubes. She swatted at his hands.

"What are you doing?"

"I thought it might ease the discomfort."

She snorted. "Discomfort? I wish I could trade places with you and let you feel this discomfort." She yanked her hand free, then grabbed his hand again as another contraction hit. Mike figured he might need a cast when this was all said and done.

His thoughts drifted to Jane, and he wondered if she was still out there, or if she'd gotten bored and gone home.

"I hate Hale," Sara said, regaining his attention.

He looked from their hands to her face and saw tears in her eyes.

A tear rolled down her cheek. "I thought he loved me, but the moment he found out I was pregnant, he vanished. Abandoned us both. What kind of man does that?"

"The kind that's scared." Another micro-ounce of

weight lifted from his chest, and even though he knew he'd never forgive himself for what he'd done, he tried to explain it to Sara. "Have you ever wondered why I fell apart after Hannah died?"

Sara's face contorted in pain and she squeezed his hand until the contraction eased. But when it was over, she continued to hold his hand gently and gave him a tired smile. "Sure. Everyone did. You've always been so strong and sure of yourself that doing what you did was totally out of character."

He kissed her fingertips and gave her a sad smile. "I might have handled Hannah's death better if I'd stayed away from the booze. Lesson learned."

"What does this have to do with Hale leaving me?"

"He was scared, Sara."

She frowned. "Well, I was scared too. Freaking out scared. I had to tell my dad and I was terrified he'd disown me. Hale should have stuck around to take part of the blame."

"Have you thought about what you'll do if he comes back?"

Another contraction snatched away her reply. She squeezed his hand and breathed through the pain, and when it passed, she laid her head back on the pillow and gazed at him, eyes narrowed and suspicious. "You're going to tell me to forgive him, aren't you?"

"Why not? You're both still kids. Until you forgive him, and he forgives himself, neither of you will ever be able to move on."

Her gaze cleared and focused on him with an intensity that reminded him of her mother. "Whose forgiveness do you need, Mike?"

With the focus back on his issues, he shifted and gave

an uncomfortable laugh. "Everyone's?"

George stepped into the room, interrupting their conversation, and examined Sara again. With a smile, he addressed her. "It's time to move to the delivery room. Do you realize that I delivered you and now I'm delivering your baby?"

"Yeah, great," Sara mumbled. "Entertain me with the story sometime when it doesn't hurt so darn much."

Mike tugged his hand out of the young woman's grip and stepped back to give the staff room to work, and Hannah's words whispered through his brain, so he repeated them. "When you're holding your precious bundle in your arms, every moment of discomfort you've had during your pregnancy, every painful contraction you've experienced, will be replaced with a love you never imagined possible."

He thought of Laura and Lisa...and prayed it wasn't too late to fix things.

CHAPTER TEN

Jane stood awkwardly in the waiting area and wondered what she should do.

All around her, people hustled and bustled with purpose and a destination, no one paying her the least bit of attention until she caught the eye of the receptionist.

The young woman smiled at her. "Is there something I can help you with?"

Jane shook her head and forced a smile. "Just waiting for a friend."

"There's a coffee shop down the hall to your left."

"Thank you." She glanced in that direction, and noted the amount of people going in and out. Too many people. Someone might recognize her. "I'll—uh—maybe I'll just sit out here."

"No problem. If there's anything I can help you with, just let me know." A spark of curiosity lit the young woman's eyes and she frowned. "Do I know you?"

"No, I don't think so." She ducked her head, but it was too late. Even before she turned her back on the girl, she saw the receptionist's eyes grow wide with horrified recognition.

She hurried to the seating area where she plopped down on a chair, tugged her hair out of its ponytail, and let it fall around her face.

In hindsight, she shouldn't have come into town with Mike and Sara, but the young girl's plight had carried her from the ranch house, into the truck, then into the hospital before she had time to think of the consequences.

Even as she sat there, head down, gaze focused on her phone, she could feel the stares of the people as they walked past.

How long would it be before another stranger recognized her? She could ignore the stares—almost. It was worse when they felt compelled to strike up a conversation with her as though they were her best friend, asking for details like a sick idiot.

Someone sat down next to her and she brushed the curtain of her hair to completely cover her profile. And then that person let out a quiet, familiar sigh.

She raised her head. "Mom, what are you doing here?"

Barbara shrugged out of her winter jacket and draped it over her shoulders, appearing nonchalant, but Jane knew otherwise. She was here to protect her youngest daughter. "Well, I couldn't miss out on all the fun. Have you heard how the delivery is going?"

"No. Nothing yet." Jane glanced at the time on her phone. Barely an hour had passed since Sara's water had broke. She straightened up from her slouched position and scooted to the front of the seat. "Why don't we go home and wait? I'll text Mike and tell him I caught a ride with you. He can call you to let you know how everything went."

"Nonsense. I have nothing better to do." Barbara patted

her knee. "Sit back and relax, honey. This is Sara's first time, so it'll probably be hours before we hear anything."

Jane brushed her hair forward again and peered around at the growing number of people settling into the seating area. She lowered her voice. "Mom, someone will recognize me."

"So?" Barbara leaned forward, cupped Jane's chin in the palm of her hand, and clucked her tongue. "I say, bring it on. You have me here to protect you."

"Mom, I don't want you to have to get involved—"

But her mother released her chin, pushed to her feet, and dumped her jacket and purse on the empty chair. "Stay here and watch my things. I'll go grab us a couple of coffees, then we can sit and chat. Be back in a jiff."

Jane watched her mom scurry away and disappear into the coffee shop. Then ducking her head again, she slumped back on the seat to wait. But she knew it would take forever. Her mother knew everyone and would be compelled to ask each person how their day was going. And even though she'd decline their request to join them— after all, her pathetic daughter was sitting alone in the seating area, too terrified to make conversation with anyone else—Barbara would still politely listen to each person's story of their day.

Twenty minutes later, a record time indeed, the older woman came out of the coffee shop with two cups in her hands. Her lips were tight as though holding in words, and her lavender eyes sparked with tiny golden flames. When she reached Jane, she silently handed her both cups, grabbed her jacket and purse, then flopped down on the seat. "Some people have a lot of nerve."

Jane handed one of the cups back. "What happened?"

"Never mind," the older woman muttered as she pulled

off the plastic lid and blew on the steaming brew. Anger wafted off her in waves. Then she took Jane's hand and squeezed it. "Fine, I'll tell you. Your sister called."

The tightness in her stomach became a vice. "About?"

"She's concerned about you and Mike."

Before the older woman could do some damage, Jane pulled her hand out of her mother's bone crushing grip. "Concerned?"

"The nerve of that girl. She's worried about all of the time you've been spending with him."

"I hope you told her to mind her own business."

"Abby is afraid you're going to get hurt."

Jane played with the edge of her coffee cup. She didn't really want to talk about her sister, but there were things she needed to know. "Mom, what happened between Abby and Mike? Why does she want to keep his daughters from him?"

Barbara rolled back her head and with a sigh, stared at the ceiling as though seeking a higher guidance. "All I ever wanted from my girls was a grandchild or three. I ask you...is that too much to wish for?"

Jane gritted her teeth. "Mom, Mike and Abby?"

Her mother blinked, brought her chin back down, and met Jane's gaze. "Your sister is upset because Mike was on the rodeo circuit instead of home with Hannah. He wanted to pay off the ranch. Maybe if he'd been home more often, he would have noticed that she was ill." She hesitated, then continued. "Or maybe not. Hannah was good at hiding most things."

Poor Mike. Her sister had a vengeful personality, and with her position of power, she had absolutely authority to do as she deemed right.

A commotion at the hospital entrance drew her

attention, and two adorable little girls raced into the foyer followed by a familiar looking woman and a handsome man. Jane shoulder bumped her mom. "Who's that?"

"Mike's girls." Barbara set the coffee cup on the side table and pushed to her feet. "And that handsome devil and the woman at his side are his brother and sister-in-law."

Hannah's twin. No wonder she looked familiar.

And suddenly her hands were sweating and shaking, and she had to set the coffee cup down beside her mom's. Because she knew without a single doubt that her mother would bring the couple over to introduce them to her, even though the older woman knew she wanted to avoid people.

Jane rested her forearms on the arms of the chair and hunched forward. She glanced to her right, then to her left. Somewhere in this hospital, there had to be a place that she could hide.

But before she could suck in a breath, her mother returned.

"Honey, I want you to meet the twins. This is Laura and this is Lisa."

Jane unclenched her teeth, raised her head, and forced a smile. She instantly recognized Laura's natural shyness and Lisa's eagerness to run off and explore. They were precious and adorable, and experience told her that they were a handful, especially the one with the mischievous twinkle in her dark eyes. Lisa.

She kept her voice quiet, hoping not to draw attention to herself. "Hello girls. I'm Jane."

Lisa readily approached her and reached out to touch her hair. "Pretty."

Her smile felt less stiff. "Thank you."

While Laura shied away and hid behind her aunt's arm, Jane wished she could do the same. Instead, her mom caught her by the elbow and tugged her out of the chair.

"I don't think either of you have met my daughter, Jane."

Anticipating the worst, Jane raised her gaze from the shy twin to the woman holding the young girl's hand, while her mother continued to chat as though all participants in the group were normal.

"Honey, I'd like you to meet Gage and Harley Toryn, Mike's brother and sister-in-law."

Jane's lunch rushed up her throat and unable to speak, she stared into the clear, dark chocolate gaze of the woman now holding out her hand in the space between them.

"It's a pleasure to meet you," the petite woman said pleasantly while Jane could only stare back at her in mute anticipation and horror.

The tall man in the peripheral of her vision stepped up to his wife, put one arm around her shoulders, and nodded. "It's great to finally meet you, Jane. We're very thankful for the help you've been giving my brother."

Jane stared into his dark blue eyes and saw nothing but kindness there. She opened her mouth to thank him, but only a squeak came out.

Then the shy twin tugged at her aunt's hand and whispered, "I have to go to the bathroom."

And when Harley dropped her hand and Lisa began to jump up and down and shout, "Me too. Me too," the movement and sound broke through Jane's fear and gave her time to gather up her defenses again.

As though no one noticed her lapse of self-control, Mike's brother scooped up his noisy niece. "Quiet, Munchkin, or you'll wake the bodies in the morgue."

The girl's eyes grew to saucers and she cupped the big man's face between her hands. "Can we see the ghosts,

Unca Gage?"

"No, it's off limits, but if you're a good girl—and by that, I mean no running and screaming—we'll watch the Ghostbuster movie tonight before bed."

With her thumb and forefinger, she pressed her lips together and nodded vigorously, her long ringlet curls bobbing around her shoulders and back.

Gage set the girl down on her feet and gave Jane a wry grin. "This is one of the benefits of being a man with two girls. No bathroom duties."

Grabbing Lisa's hand before she could escape, Harley gave him a saucy grin. "Which is why we're having boys, my love." Before she turned away, the other woman paused and looked straight at Jane. "If you don't mind, Jane, I could use the help. My husband can keep your mom company."

"Uh, sure," she breathed and feet lagging, she followed the other woman and prepared herself for the inquisition ahead.

Except that it never came, or at least, not in the manner she expected.

Inside the bathroom, the girls disappeared into the empty stalls, and Harley faced Jane.

"So is it true? You're helping Mike?" At Jane's silence, Harley gave a sheepish grin. "It's a small community. Also, Barbara called. She likes to keep me informed about Mike."

Self-conscious and still braced for the other woman's judgment, Jane shrugged. "I hope you don't mind. He needed help and I'm available."

"Mind?" There was so much relief in the petite woman's tone that Jane relaxed a smidgen more. "Of course not. It makes me happy that he has someone in his corner. We've all been so worried about him." She slid a glance toward the bathroom stalls, and lowered her voice. "The girls miss him something terrible, but every day they're apart, they forget who their parents are and bond closer with Gage and me. It's not an ideal situation, but that's how it is."

Jane blinked. She'd forgotten what it was like to have a normal conversation with someone else, nearly forgotten what it was like to put someone else's needs before her own fear. But she knew the other woman was right. Every day Mike was separated from his young daughters was a day they couldn't get back. "So you wouldn't object to Mike regaining custody of his girls?"

"Not at all. We want what's best for all of them, and being together is what's best."

"Tell that to my sister," she muttered. "Mike saw Abby and she turned down his request."

"I know. She called. I would have called him so we could work something out, but things have been strained between us since my sister's passing."

"Aunt Harley," one of the girls called from inside the cubicle. "I don't have any toilet paper."

Soon, Harley had persuaded Lisa to pass her sister some toilet paper, and a couple of minutes later, the girls came barreling out of the stalls. Jane helped Lisa wash her hands while Harley did the same with Laura.

Back in the waiting room, as time ticked by and the girls grew more restless, Jane watched her mother and Harley take turns trying to entertain them. And she hoped they were all still there when Mike came out of the delivery room so the healing could begin.

Outside the window, she saw a truck swerve into the parking lot and Sara's parents climbed out. She watched the hunky cowboy escort his wife inside. The man doted on her like she was the queen of everything in his world, and Jane had to struggle against the jealousy that flared up. She'd never experienced that kind of love, the kind that consumed a person until the two became one.

She turned her back on the window, feeling awkward and out of place and self-conscious, and gazed around the room at Mike's relatives and friends.

Did he know how lucky he was to have them in his life? They didn't seem to care who she was—or most probably, like Mike, they just didn't know—and they treated her as though she were normal. But sooner or later, one of them would make the connection and then they'd all shun her like a fox attempting to sneak into the chicken coop.

A scream erupted from one of the twins, drawing her attention, and she turned in time to see the one she identified as Lisa kick her sister who immediately turned and kicked her back. Deciding to give the other two women a break, Jane approached the twins. "Did anyone bring some crayons and coloring books?"

The group went silent, including the twins who immediately stopped bickering and stared up at her with interest.

Harley sighed as she slid a glance toward her husband. "We rushed out of the house so fast, we didn't think to pack anything to entertain them. *#parentingfailure*."

Gage raked his fingers through his hair and gave the twins a lopsided grin. "You'd think by now we'd have this parenting gig figured out."

Laura scooted across the floor and put her arms around his neck. "It's okay, Uncle Gage. You're doing the best you can."

As he hugged her back, Jane crouched down to the

twins' level. "If it's okay with your aunt and uncle, I'll take you to the hospital gift shop, and we can pick up some coloring books and crayons."

"Jane is a kindergarten teacher," her mother inserted into the conversation. "She has lots of ideas for keeping the children entertained. In fact, she tells me she's quite fond of this age." Her mother gave her a wry glance. "Which doesn't explain why I don't have any grandkids yet, does it?"

"Not helping, Mom." She turned to Harley. "We'll go straight to the gift shop and back. No side trips. I promise."

Gage stood and reached into his pocket. "I'll pay."

As Jane straightened, she shook her head and backed away, holding out a hand to each girl. "My treat."

"Thank you," the couple said in unison.

With a girl clinging to each hand, she steered them toward the gift shop.

Laura, the quiet one, gazed up at her. "Lisa doesn't color inside the lines."

Lisa grinned and skipped along on her other side. "Coloring inside lines is for sissies."

"Is not," Laura grumbled.

Jane smiled down at the older twin. "It takes practice, but you know, sometimes it's fun to color outside of the lines."

Ahead of them, she saw Jessie Adams and Nate Coltrane run into the hospital, and stop at the reception desk.

And as she turned the corner toward the gift shop, she wondered how Sara was making out...and if Mike was still with her or if he'd run away again.

CHAPTER ELEVEN

Within the hour, Sara's daughter was delivered, healthy, and with a set of lungs that would have rivaled her great-grandma, Maude. A few minutes after the delivery, the nurse took Mike by the arm and steered him toward the door.

"We'd like to clean Sara and the baby up. Go grab a coffee and something to eat and take a break." She smiled at him, warm and friendly and totally oblivious to the fact that he was a man who let people down. "You did great in there. Sara is lucky to have you in her life."

"Thanks," he mumbled. He glanced back at the new mother who had turned to watch him being escorted out. "See you later, kid."

Sara gave him a weary smile. "I couldn't have done this without you, Mike."

"It's the most fun I've had in eons. I wouldn't have missed it for the world." He grinned when she snorted, then sobered. "I'm glad I could be here for you, kid."

As he headed out of the room, he heard her whispered *thank you* and his throat thickened.

Sara had one hundred and fifty percent of her parents' support, and he had little doubt that she would ever need his assistance again. But after going through the labour and delivery with her, he felt responsible for both mother and child. And he knew that he would do anything for them.

He headed down the long hallway toward the waiting room and saw Jessie hurrying his way, a white gown covering her street clothes, a mask in her hands. When she reached him she stopped, her worried gaze searching his.

"How is Sara? The baby?"

Mike gave her a reassuring smile. "You have a beautiful little granddaughter, Jessie. They're cleaning them both up right now."

"You were with her the entire time?" At his nod, her eyes filled with tears, and she stepped into him and wrapped her arms around his shoulders. Her voice broke. "Thank you for taking care of my baby. I'm glad you were there."

Surprised, he gave her a hug back. "I'm glad I could help. You would have been proud of her. She was strong and brave and didn't complain once."

She hugged him again, then released him, and with tears in her eyes, gently cupped the side of his face before she hurried off to see her daughter.

Mike stared after her for a moment before he resumed his trek to the waiting room where he stopped before he headed in. He glanced down at his attire, noticed that he still wore the gown the hospital had given him, and pulled it off. Jamming his hat on his head, he eyed the interior of the room.

He saw his brother first, comfortable and casual and easy as he stood in the middle of the room talking to Nate. He had a gold band on the third finger of his left hand.

Had he attended Gage's wedding? He tried to squeeze the memory out of his brain, but the last few months were a fuzzy blur with only the most retched memories highlighted and staying.

He saw his sister-in-law second, and when his gaze wanted to slither past how much she looked like her twin sister, past how painful it was to look at her now and remember what it had been like with the only woman he'd ever loved, he forced himself to look at her face. His heart hiccuped and guilt consumed him.

She'd avoided him since the incident, and he'd avoided her, but Mike knew he couldn't continue to do so, not if he wanted to heal their relationship.

She turned her head to peer up at her husband and her dark hair swept her shoulders with the movement, a movement that reminded him so much of her sister, all he wanted to do was close the distance between them, embrace her, and lose himself in the memory of everything he'd once had.

But he'd screwed things up because he'd confused them before, and now it was up to him to make amends.

His attention shifted past his sister-in-law, past Jane who sat hunched at the child-sized table poking through the crayons, and finally to his girls.

Laura twirled the lock of hair that hung over her eyes, and swung one leg back and forth under the table while she concentrated solely on the coloring book.

Lisa had her tongue hanging out of her mouth, and even from this distance, he could see that she was coloring outside the lines and loving it.

He'd once known every nuance of their personality and quirks, and loved being privy to the new ones they developed.

If his heart hiccuped when he saw Harley, his heart now stuttered and paused before it began to race in his chest, and the raw pain of his separation from the twins sliced him to ribbons. The back of his eyes burned, but he couldn't fall apart now, not right before he came face-to-face with his family, so he gritted his teeth and shoved everything down deep where no one could see it.

The thought of taking care of them alone scared the hell out of him, but he knew that he'd do whatever it took. For the first time ever, he saw how much they were going to look like their mother when they grew up. And the pain that was with him twenty-four hours a day eased a tiny bit more.

"Hannah? Honey?" he whispered into the quiet corridor. "Can you see them? I promise you, I'll figure this out and I won't make a mess of it again."

As he pulled his attention from the twins, his gaze collided with Jane. She'd stopped coloring to watch him, compassion in her eyes. His cheeks heated. Palm flat against the door, he pushed it open and stepped inside.

The second the adults in the room noticed him, all conversation died. Not wanting to seem too eager—or too scared—he crossed to the middle of the room.

Gage shifted over to make room for him, and with a smile, clapped him on the back. "Heard you nearly had to deliver a baby in your truck."

Nate pulled him in for a bear hug, his voice thick with tears. "Thanks, bud. I don't think I can ever repay you for taking care of Sara when Jessie and I couldn't be there for her."

"You'd do the same for me." He awkwardly hugged Nate back, and as he released his friend, the pain Mike had been hiding from burst free in his chest, robbing him of his breath. Behind him, a door swished open, and George's voice caught the attention of the other two men before they noticed Mike's breakdown.

He swiped a hand across his eyes. He could blame it on the tension of the last few hours, but the truth of the matter was that helping Sara through the birth made him miss his daughters even more.

George still wore his green scrubs and he had a huge smile on his face. He headed straight for Nate, grabbed his hand, pumped his arm, and clapped his hand on his shoulder. "Congratulations, you're now the proud grandpa of a beautiful baby girl."

Nate grabbed George in a bear hug, then released him. "How are they doing? When can I see them?"

George's grin widened. "They're both doing great. Emma's a wee bit early so we'll keep her under observation for a few days, but I have no concerns at this point. You can see them both in a few minutes. The staff will be moving them to a room soon and I'll have them come get you when they're ready."

Nate hugged him again and pulled a cigar out of his pocket. "Here, you deserve this."

As George's pager went off, he backed up a step. "Save it for later. I need to get back to work."

As the doctor left and Nate began to pass out cigars, Mike heard his oldest daughter's voice. Laura had raised her gaze from the coloring book and had focused on his sister-in-law.

"Is Uncle Gage putting a baby in your tummy, Aunt Harley?"

"Someday, honey," their aunt replied with a wink at her husband.

Mike raised one brow and glanced toward his brother.

"What kind of things are you teaching them?"

Uncle Gage sighed. "Your daughters are like sponges. They also have the ability to appear at the most awkward of moments."

Nate smirked. "So when *are* you putting a baby in your wife's tummy?"

Gage grinned and lowered his voice. "We haven't told anyone yet, because we're still waiting for confirmation, but we're pretty sure we're pregnant."

Mike clapped him on the shoulder, some of the tension easing as he remembered that these two men were his *family*. "Congratulations."

"Don't tell anyone else."

Nate winked. "Just Jessie. We don't keep secrets from one another."

Gage grumbled under his breath. "Just tell her to act surprised when Harley springs the news."

A nurse showed up at the door. "Nate, Emma is ready to meet you now."

The cowboy grandpa was gone in a flash.

In his absence, an awkward silence fell over the room. Mike didn't know what to say, but he realized he was glad Gage and Harley had stepped in. No man was an island. He should know. He'd tried to be one for Hannah, and in the end, by not allowing family and friends into that part of his life when he could have used their support the most, he'd nearly ruined everything.

He faced his brother, open and honest instead of in hiding. "Thank you. I'm glad you and Harley were there for the twins. I may have been an ass about it at the time, but you did what you needed to do to keep them safe."

Gage shrugged, relief in his gaze. "That's what family's for." There was a pause during which he glanced at his wife, then back at him. "When do you think you'll be ready to take the girls back?"

Mike straightened, surprised by the question. "After all I've done—to the girls, to Harley, and to you—you'd still trust me with them?"

"They're your daughters." His brother's gaze was serious and considering. "And it's not like I won't keep an eye on you."

He'd thought it would be months before his brother and sister-in-law released them into his care.

He'd thought he'd have to beg for their return.

So at the moment, Mike didn't care if Gage moved into the spare bedroom in the ranch house, as long as the twins returned home where they belonged.

"I talked to Abby yesterday, but she turned me down," he admitted as the full import of the girls returning home hit him. He tugged at the collar of his shirt and shifted on his feet. "I'm ready, I think…almost."

Gage laid one hand on his shoulder, his voice low, his steely gaze serious. "Don't fall apart on me, bro."

"I won't." He gazed into his older brother's eyes and hoped his sincerely showed in his own. "I promise, I've straightened out. And Jane's been over every day helping me get ready. We've got the house cleaned up, the pantry restocked, and the fridge full. There's no reason why they couldn't come home now. Today." He gave a nervous laugh. "I'm being over anxious, aren't I?"

"I'd be the same," Gage reassured him. "What about you, man? Do you think you can handle them?"

Mike nodded. "I know you probably need more proof than this, but I give you my word, I won't screw up again."

"If Nate were here, he'd tell you that you're bound to screw up multiple times, but that the important thing is that you love them and forgive them despite *their* screw ups."

"Of which there are sure to be many." He eyed his brother. "You're going to make a great dad."

"I'm certainly going to try my damnedest." He raised his eyebrows and lowered his voice. "By the way, you owe Harley an apology."

"I owe her way more than that." Mike glanced her way. "Will she mind if I talk to her?"

"I know she'd appreciate it." Gage paused, then added, "Hannah was her sister. She was grieving too."

Guilt infused Mike. He nodded, then turned toward his sister-in-law. As he approached, she pushed to her feet, her expression fierce and protective and so loving, it nearly slayed him. This woman was so totally opposite of her sweet, gentle sister that he wondered how he'd ever confused them. No wonder he'd made such a mess of things.

His gaze skittered off her face again down to his youngest daughter as Lisa slid off her chair and came to stand beside her aunt. A moment later, Laura joined them, her eyes somber and wary.

Harley glanced down at the twins, then back up at him. "Hello, Mike. I hear you've had quite the day."

He forced a smile and hoped it didn't look as phony as it felt. "Sara did all of the work and she did great. All I did was give her something to break." He held up his hand, but his joke fell flat when Harley didn't smile. So he lowered his hand to his side. "I owe you an apology."

Without hesitation, she said, "Apology accepted."

"Thank you." His gaze sliced to the twins, then back to his sister-in-law's face. "Do you mind if I say hi to the girls?"

At her sharp nod, he crouched down to the girls' level.

"Hi Laura. Hi Lisa."

The twins pressed closer to their aunt. Laura spoke first. "Daddy?"

"Hi, baby." His voice broke and he had to clear his throat before he continued. "I've missed you girls."

Lisa stuck her thumb in her mouth and started sucking on it hard.

Harley pulled it out, then gave the twins a gentle push forward. "Give your daddy a hug, girls."

But they resisted, planting the rubber soles of their tiny pink sneakers against the tiled floor, leaning back against their aunt's hands, refusing to budge.

The silence grew heavy and Mike knew his sister-in-law was waiting for him to make the next move. He cleared the hoarseness from his throat. "I've missed you girls. You've both grown taller." When the silence continued, he continued. "Your horses miss you too. Do you miss them?"

At least this time Lisa appeared interested. "Our *horsies?*"

He focused on his youngest daughter and smiled. "Are you looking forward to riding again?"

Lisa tugged at Harley's hand and craned her neck upward. "Can we, Mommy? Can we?"

Her words were like a blow to his gut and he realized that everything Nate had said was true. He noticed his brother as he joined the united front, saw Laura let go of Harley's hand and tuck her hand into his, leaning into him, half hiding her tiny face behind his large hand.

Mike slowly gained his feet, feeling like the biggest loser—and the worst dad—in the whole world. He pulled off his hat, slapped it against his leg, uncertain what to try next...or if he should even bother.

Gage slung one arm over Harley's shoulders, casual

and comfortable and so obviously in love, Mike had to look away before he started to cry. "Well, Aunt Harley, what do you say?"

This is how his own life had been, so in love with the woman he'd married that he'd never looked at another woman ever again. So in love with the woman of his dreams that all he'd seen in their future was laughter and joy. So in love with his wife that for the first time ever, he'd believed in happily-ever-after.

But it had been a fallacy. Life was too short for some and too mean for others, and it was far better to hide his head in a bottle of booze and forget than it was to remember how good he'd once had it.

And yet, the people who'd saved his twin daughters from him now faced him, united in their effort to save him from his grief. But it would never happened. He'd promised to love Hannah forever and he'd keep that promise till his dying breath, when he could hopefully be reunited with her.

He felt a warm hand fold into his and the contact brought him back from the edge of despair. When he glanced down and saw Jane at his side, something eased in his chest.

She was smiling at the twins. "Would you girls like to come out to the ranch and visit the horses? I'm there every day, so you'll see me too."

The girls exchanged a glance, then peered up at their aunt and uncle. Laura asked, "Uncle Gage, could we go?"

He nodded and focused his sympathetic gaze on Mike. "How does tomorrow afternoon work?"

"Perfectly," he replied, forcing his gaze off the twins.

"Then it's a date," Harley stated. She prodded the twins toward him again. "Why don't you girls give your daddy a hug?"

He was surprised again, but he wasn't surprised when the twins withdrew further. Softly, he said, "I love you both very, very much, and I have a lot to make up for."

He saw tears in Harley's eyes, and when she looked like she was about to force the issue, he shrugged. "No worries, Harley. I can wait till they're ready."

His oldest daughter tugged at Gage's hand, her chubby face tilted up so she could peer at him through the unruly curl impeding her vision, her voice a stage whisper. "Can we go home now, Uncle Gage? Lisa is scared of the bad daddy."

Mike forced himself to take a step back, his smile firmly in place while his heart broke in two. "I'll see you all tomorrow. The horses will be ready."

He met his brother's eyes, then his sister-in-law's gaze, and attempted to telegraph a message.

It's okay. I can deal with this.

And as he watched them walk away, the twins visibly relaxing as they put distance between them and their *bad daddy*, Jane squeezed his hand and leaned into his side.

"You okay?"

"Yeah, sure." When the twins were out of sight, he turned his head, and found himself falling into the liquid warmth of her soft gaze. "I knew it wouldn't be easy."

She squeezed his hand again, then with a flush to her cheeks, let go and stepped away. "It'll take time, but you'll get there, and I'm not going anywhere until you do."

Barbara joined them and with tears in her lavender eyes, gave him a hug. "They love you, they've just forgotten that they do."

He gave a self-conscious laugh and scrubbed the moisture from his eyes. "Thank you. Both of you."

"If you need anything, Mike, you just call Walter or me." His kindly neighbor turned to her daughter. "Well, honey, we best head home before your father begins to think I've abandoned him."

With a wave, she headed toward the exit, leaving Mike alone with Jane who shuffled her feet before she pulled her gaze from her mother and turned to him. She gave him an awkward smile. "So I guess I'll see you tomorrow."

He could feel her discomfort wafting off her in waves, and only then did he remember how uncomfortable she seemed to be around people. Scrubbing a hand over the back of his neck, he frowned. "Jane, you don't have to get involved."

She shrugged and started to back away, a small smile playing on her mouth. "The twins are sweet. It'll be fun."

Then she turned and displaying remarkable agility, dodged the couple behind her, sprinted after her mother, and disappeared outside.

At a slower pace, Mike followed her out, his instincts once again warning him that not all was right with Jane. Perhaps it was time to come right out and ask Barbara what had happened.

From across the parking lot came the sound of a child's squeal of delight, and Mike's thoughts returned to his daughters. He had options.

He could leave the girls right where they were, comfortable with Gage and Harley. It was clear the couple dearly loved them.

But they were his daughters, his responsibility.

And from here on out, in order to regain their love and trust, he had to be the best daddy ever.

CHAPTER TWELVE

Early the next morning, Jane rode Pepper across the field, heading south to the Rocky Creek Ranch.

The air was crisp and cold, and overnight the combination of the freezing temperature and high humidity had draped the spruce and poplar trees with hoar frost that twinkled in the bright sunlight.

In the distance, a fox scampered across the white fields, pausing to paw at a snow covered mound, searching for its next meal. She watched it until it disappeared over a small rise in the ground, leaving her alone with the stillness and the quiet.

This is what she had needed when she'd come home. The soft crunch of the snow beneath Pepper's hooves, her breath steamy in the cold air, the panoramic view of the snow covered Rocky Mountains in the distance.

Her phone vibrated against her chest, and she reined in her horse, tugged off one glove, and reached inside her jacket to pull out the device. Fully expecting to see a text from her mother or Mike, the name on the screen ripped her back to the reality of her life.

They're in the process of selecting the jury.

She stared down at the screen.

For a short time, she'd managed to forget about the recent past and the unforeseeable future, but now she realized that it wouldn't go away, not ever.

Becoming suddenly aware that she was alone and vulnerable, she glanced at the vast emptiness around her, and nudged Pepper forward.

Her phone vibrated again.

We need you, Jane. If you don't testify, he'll walk.

Maybe if she didn't reply, the lawyer would eventually give up and go away. Inhaling the icy air into her lungs, she powered down the phone and tucked the device back into the inside pocket of her jacket. After what seemed like an eternity during which she jumped at every shadow and noise, she reached the Rocky Creek Ranch. Spotting Mike through the trees, she tugged on the reins and Pepper stopped.

Fear clenched at her stomach and settled heavy in her chest, making it difficult to draw in a breath. The urge to turn back toward the safety of her parents overwhelmed her.

"It's okay," she whispered to herself. "He doesn't see me as a woman. He's still in love with his wife. With Hannah."

The certainty of her statement calmed her down—just barely—and Jane finally urged Pepper forward. As she rode into the yard, Mike raised his head. There was so much relief on his face, she was suddenly glad she hadn't chickened out and turned back.

She rode right up to him, and he caught the reins of the horse and smiled.

"You made it. I was beginning to think you'd changed

your mind."

Jane forced herself to return his smile. "What? And spend the day staring at the walls of my bedroom?"

As she swung her leg over to dismount, he reached for her and she reactively tensed. She hung there in the air, one foot in the stirrup, half dismounted, his hands clasping her waist.

Holding her prisoner. Forcing her to his will.

A scream expanded her chest...then vanished as he released her and backed several feet away. She sensed his gaze on her back, intense and curious. And as she swallowed back the fear and came the rest of the way down, embarrassment heated her cold cheeks and flushed her body.

She slowly turned to face him, barely able to make eye contact, her hands shaking so badly, she had to stuff them into her jacket pockets to hide them. She forced herself to take a deep breath, and with a forced laugh and an eye roll, she said, "Ignore me. I'm an idiot."

Holding his gaze, she waited for the inquisition, recognized the moment when he made the choice to let it go.

A huge weight lifted off her chest. Her secret was safe, for the time being. She forced another smile, this one less stiff. "How are you doing?"

"Nervous as hell," he admitted as he shifted forward, careful to keep his distance as he took hold of the reins of the horse. "It's worse than a blind date or a job interview."

She pushed back the cuff of her jacket and peered at her watch, knowing full well the answer to her question, but wanting to make conversation so that neither of them had time to dwell on the fact that she'd nearly fallen to pieces. "What time will they be here again?"

"Ten." As he reached the entrance to the stables, he glanced over his shoulder, down the driveway, emitting nervousness like she expelled fear.

She felt sorry for him. Sorry that he'd lost his wife, lost his daughters, and had to go through this. She relaxed a bit more. "Why don't we get the horses ready?"

He pulled his gaze from the driveway, entered the horse barn, and tied Pepper to a post. Jane followed along behind him.

"I was headed to do that when you rode in." Lifting the saddle flap, he unbuckled the girth and lifted the saddle off the horse's back. "Meet Belle and Ariel."

While Mike led Pepper to one of the stalls, and removed the bridle and reins, Jane wandered toward the ponies on the opposite side of the aisle. They were smaller than Pepper, not quite full grown, perfect for the twins. She ran one hand down the nose of one, then the other. "Oh, I get it. Disney."

"Yep."

He grabbed a small saddle off the wall and she crossed the room to grab the other. The heavy silence and Mike's pinched brow bothered her, so she randomly picked a safe topic. "How did you get into the cowboy business?"

"I worked for Nate's dad one summer and fell in love with the lifestyle."

She snort-laughed. "Manure and muck?"

Her question elicited a grin and he paused, rested one hand on the saddle to peer at her. There was a moment when he appeared self-conscious. Then it was gone. "It's the peace and quiet. Sometimes I stop working just to listen to the sounds of nature."

She understood. "The birds chirping, the creek running in the distance, the crackle of the northern lights. You can't get that in the city."

He raised one brow. "And yet, that's where you live."

She shrugged. "Some people say the mountains are too closed in for them, but they make me feel safe."

He nodded and went back to work on the saddle, adjusting the straps for the twins. "Hannah never really liked living in the country. She supported my need to live here, but she always talked about one day moving back to town."

Jane stopped. "Really?"

"Yeah." His voice grew gruff. "Until near the end. She liked to sit on the porch in the quiet of the early morning and look out at the vast mountain range. I think it brought her closer to Heaven or God or whatever she believed in."

Her voice was soft. "I'm glad she found peace." She saw him brush moisture away from his eyes and she changed the topic. "So what's your plan with the girls today?"

He finished cinching up the saddle, then came to help her because she'd been talking instead of doing. "A ride, then lunch. Maybe when they see their bedroom, they'll start to soften toward the idea of coming home." He rested one hand on the seat of the saddle. "I failed them when they needed me the most. I failed Hannah too. She counted on me to take care of the girls for her. I don't think I'll ever be able to forgive myself for that."

Without thought, Jane covered his hand with hers, aware that he was letting down his guard. "It does no good to dwell on the past. You can only do the right thing now, Mike."

He turned his hand over and caught hers, and she stared at his warm hand holding hers so gently. Her heart began to flutter.

The man was sweet and kind and oh so dangerous.

She started to withdraw from his touch, but his question arrested her movement.

"What happened to you, Jane?"

Could she trust him with her secret? A secret that would eventually come out when she stepped onto the witness stand and told her story.

She'd never dreamed that she could trust a man again, but here she was, halfway there. And it felt...almost right.

She was supposed to be helping *him* out, not the other way around. He'd already been through so much, and if he discovered her secret, he'd push her away.

And she wouldn't blame him a single bit.

She forced herself to look him straight in the eye. "Nothing happened to me."

His gaze remained fixed on her face. "Then why are you here hiding? What are you running from?"

She opened her mouth to say—well, she wasn't quite sure what she *could* say—when the sound of a vehicle penetrated the roar in her ears.

Jane tugged her hand free and cinched the saddle so hard, the pony bucked. She stepped back and grabbed the pony's reins. "They're here. Let's go have some fun."

"You never need to be afraid of me. I would never hurt you." Mike flicked a glance toward the doorway, then refocused on her, intense and somber. "Your secret is safe with me, honey. I'm a great secret keeper."

But she wasn't safe with him, she thought as she turned on her heel, tied the pony to a post, and fled the barn into the chilly air and warm sunshine.

Jane could hear Mike follow her at a slower pace and knew...

If she let down her guard, if she told him the truth and

revealed the awful, dirty details of her months in captivity, he would never allow her near him or his family again.

CHAPTER THIRTEEN

Mike followed Jane out into the crisp morning air and felt the warmth of the sun heat his face. He was willing to let it alone for now, but he sensed her desperate need to talk.

Whatever had happened had been bad and he knew he shouldn't get involved. He had enough on his plate with trying to get custody of the girls, but then he remembered how he'd shut everyone out and subsequently imploded.

And he couldn't allow Jane to do that and live with himself in the aftermath.

He made a mental note to call Abby later. The social worker might not like him, but she loved her sister.

Taking a deep breath, Mike dragged his attention from the puzzling woman ahead of him to the little family getting out of Harley's Volkswagen.

Gage climbed out of the driver's side, unfolding his tall frame from the tiny interior while Harley, in mid-laugh, disembarked from the passenger side. Mike felt the pinch of pain that he always felt when he saw his sister-in-law, and he wondered if it would ever go away.

And then the girls came tumbling out of the back seat

and fell into the snow, laughing and giggling and making snow angels in their brand new matching pink snow suits. His heart expanded with so much love, for a moment, he was unable to draw a breath.

Then Jane was there beside him, her brow furrowed, her voice soft, his questions about *her* problems forgotten in the face of *his* problems.

She tugged on his coat sleeve. "Mike, come greet your daughters."

He blinked and forced his leaden legs to carry him across to Harley first, and he greeted her with a hug. "Thank you for bringing them."

"You're welcome," she breathed, and by the surprise in her voice, he'd nearly shocked the speech from her.

He went to his brother, the man who had rescued the twins and Harley from him, and pulled him into a hug...not just a handshake this time. As the two men broke apart, he realized the twins were back on their feet, eying him with trepidation.

Mike smiled down at them, hope in his heart, enthusiasm in his voice. "Who's up for a pony ride?"

Laura put her hands behind her back and stared down at her feet.

Lisa boldly stepped forward, and eyes squinted, face puckered, shouted, *"You're a meanie."*

Harley shot forward, her pixie features twisted with shock. "Lisa Toryn, don't you dare talk to your daddy like that."

"It's okay, Harley, I deserved that." Mike focused on his daughter, sorrow in his heart, and tried to be nonchalant. "So I guess you don't want to see Ariel then?"

The puckered face of his youngest daughter morphed into a tooth-filled grin and she crossed her eyes at him.

"Course I do, silly Daddy."

Gage ruffled her hair. "Manners, Munchkin."

"Yes, Unca Gage," she sang out gaily as she grabbed his hand and gazed up at her uncle with such adoration, Mike wondered if she would ever look at him that way again. "May I pretty please ride Ariel?"

Gage gently extracted his hand from hers and nudged her toward Mike. "I'm not the horse guy. You'll have to go with your daddy."

Mike turned his attention to his oldest daughter. "What about you, Laura?"

Arms crossed over her chest, mutiny twisting her tiny mouth, Laura ignored him and glared up at her uncle. "Can we *please* go home now?"

Gage grimaced. "Not till we're done here."

Mike hunkered down on the ground in front of his oldest daughter. "This is your home, Laura. Don't you want to ride Belle, then maybe see some of your things after lunch?"

But the five-year-old was determined to punish him, and with the smoothness of a teenager in mid-sulk, she turned her back on him and stomped away.

Jane stepped in and took Lisa's hand. "Let's go with your daddy, honey, and we'll see Ariel. She's all saddled for you."

"K," the younger twin agreed before her focused shifted to her sister. "Laura, are you coming?"

"*No.*"

The shouted response echoed between the buildings and reverberated between the hills and valleys of the surrounding foothills.

Mike straightened and stepped back, willing her to turn and face him, to change her mind and forgive him and

121

return home without months and months—maybe years—of begging on his part. But when she didn't, he said, "If you change your mind, Laura, Uncle Gage will bring you to the barn."

Then he turned and followed Jane and Lisa.

There was no missing the fact that the farther Lisa got from her sister and aunt and uncle, the more reluctant she felt about her decision. By the time they reached the entrance to the horse barn, Lisa was barely moving, dragging her feet as though they were caked with mud.

Mike stepped around her, entered the building, and walked down the aisle to untie the pony.

The instant Lisa saw her horse, she let go of Jane's hand and raced forward, throwing her arms around the pony's neck. "Ariel, I missed you."

Mike crouched down to her level. "Want to ride her?"

She nodded, so he reached for her, but she sidestepped him and held out her hands to Jane, demanding, "You do it."

Mike stepped back like an observer while Jane set Lisa on the saddle, then lead the pony and rider outside to the corral. He watched them, quiet and still, until Harley slipped up beside him.

She linked her arms through his. "I'm so sorry. I had hoped—"

"After what I did, I deserve it." He turned his head and met her dark mocha gaze. For a moment, it seemed like he was looking into his wife's compassionate eyes and his throat threatened to close up. "I'm the one who should be apologizing. I haven't told you how very sorry I am for what I did."

She smiled up at him. "It's done and I'm moving forward."

"But I let you down. I let your sister down. I dumped everything on your lap when it was my responsibility."

Her smile faded. Only then did it occur to him how different this woman was from his wife. Hannah had been sweet and gentle and easily hurt. But Harley had a ferocious streak that appeared whenever someone she loved was threatened.

And it came out right now. "Mike Toryn, don't make me take you down until you cry uncle."

He snorted. "I'm twice your size."

"So's your brother, but I've taken him down."

"Okay, so truce?"

"Family," she murmured, and it warmed his insides. Together they watched Lisa ride, then Harley said, "If it wasn't for you, Gage and I might never have gotten together."

"Really?"

"Uh huh. Your brother is an idiot. He didn't think he could have me or a family." Her eyes darkened and Mike wondered what they'd gone through. Maybe someday they would tell him their story. Then her eyes twinkled. "Did Gage tell you I'm pregnant?"

Radiating what he hoped was innocence, he smiled down at her. "No. Gosh, this is a total surprise. Congratulations."

"That man can't keep a secret." She laughed. "It's a spring baby. May."

He relaxed slightly. "Gage must be thrilled."

"Over the moon."

There was a smile in her voice, and for the first time ever, Mike was truly happy for his brother and sister-in-law. His voice softened. "You two are going to make amazing parents."

She glanced up at him, her eyes squinty and probing, her voice low and serious. "You do know that Hannah and you were role models for both Gage and I, don't you?"

Disbelief filled his chest with pain and he shook his head. "You don't have to be kind. I know I screwed up. I know that if Hannah had been the one left alone with the girls, the twins would have been safe and protected. You and Gage would never have had to step in."

She sighed and rolled her eyes. "Are you back to that? Believe what you will, but the truth of the matter is that you were taking care of those girls alone a long time before Hannah died, and doing a great job of it. You just can't see it yet."

Could she be right? Mike knew that he'd done the majority of the work, but his wife had been the calming influence he needed to survive each day.

Beside him, Harley pulled back, suddenly all efficient as she called out, "A few more minutes, Lisa, and then we have to leave."

Despite Lisa's loud and very dramatic, objection, Harley turned to face him. "So tomorrow, if you have nothing on your agenda, why don't you pick up the twins and me, and we'll all go do something together."

She'd caught him off guard with her suggestion. "Sure. What?"

"Surprise us." She smiled. "Gage is working, but why don't you bring Jane. The girls really seem to like her. Ten o'clock again?"

He nodded, and then she crossed to get Lisa.

After they'd said goodbye—both girls ignoring him this time—and drove away, Laura twisted in the back seat and stared out the back window at him. He wondered what she was thinking. It was probably *Good riddance* or *bad daddy*.

Well, the day hadn't gone exactly as planned. Trying to be the best dad ever to a couple of pissed off five-year-olds was going to be harder than he imagined.

Jane came to stand beside him, waving at them with one hand. "So how do you think it went?"

"Bad." As the vehicle disappeared down the driveway, he headed back to the barn to unsaddle the ponies, aware of Jane following him, pity in her gaze. "But there's still hope."

"Sometimes that's all we need to get through the rough patches." Jane had fallen into step with him as though it were the most natural thing in the world. "So now what?"

"I'm not sure. Harley suggested we get together tomorrow morning. Want to join us again?"

She appeared startled. "Why do you need me with you?"

"For moral support. To help ease the awkwardness." He cleared his throat and decided he'd gain a whole lot more of her trust if he was open and honest. "Because I'm scared?"

Her expression turned soft. "You have nothing to be afraid of. Your girls love you. You just need to show them that you love them back."

His mouth grew grim. "I didn't grow up in that kind of household. Everything I learned about being a parent, I learned from Hannah."

"Is that how your brother learned how to be a parent? From Hannah or Harley?"

He remembered his conversation with his sister-in-law, but before he could reply, Jane continued.

"Nobody knows how to be a parent until they're faced with the joy of parenthood."

"You mean two a.m. feedings and messy diapers?"

"And butterfly kisses and chubby arms around their neck."

That had been the best part of being a parent. "So you'll come with me?"

Her eyes—her beautiful eyes that reminded him of the soft purple hues of a mid-summer sunset—lit up. "Sure. What will we do?"

Silent, he considered their options while he undid the first saddle, hefted it off the pony, and carried it across the aisle. He noticed then that Jane was in the process of saddling her own horse.

He'd thought about asking her to stay for lunch…maybe supper too. It got lonely on the ranch and she was easy to talk to. Too easy. And the realization that he was attracted to her caught him off guard.

Mike turned to the second pony, knowing full well that inviting her to stay was a bad idea, especially knowing how uneasy she was whenever she was alone with him. He focused on tomorrow. "What about a visit with Sara and Emma?"

Across the aisle, her bruised eyes lit up with delight. "The girls will love it."

"Great. I'll give Sara a call to make sure it's okay. Either way, I'll pick you up at nine-thirty, if that's okay."

"You bet." As she mounted her horse, she sat high up on the saddle and looked down at him. "Thank you for including me."

He tipped his hat at her. "No problem. Thank you for helping me with the girls so much."

Nudging the horse with her heels, she rode away, leaving him alone with the peace and quiet of the ranch…and hope where there'd been none before.

Mike pulled out his cell, confirmed the visit with Sara

who was back at home with her parents already, then worked until sundown when he headed to the bunkhouse and showered. After having a quick bite to eat, he picked up the blanket Hannah had crocheted, wrapped it around his shoulders, and sat down on the rocker that she'd once used to rock their babies to sleep. Sometimes it brought him comfort, especially when he could feel the warmth of her body as though she'd just gotten up from it.

Nights like tonight, when his heart felt heaviest and his future appeared bleaker and lonelier than ever, he wondered what he'd done to deserve his fate. Why his wife, the love of his life and the mother of his two sweet little girls, had been taken instead of him.

He peered around the room and whispered, "Hey baby, are you still here?"

Silence slipped around him and left him colder than before.

Maybe he was a little crazy, talking to the dead, but he tried again anyway. His voice dropped even lower. "I miss you, baby. I miss your sweet smile and holding you in my arms. Every day without you is killing me."

But even as he said it, the image of Jane popped into his thoughts. Jane frozen at his touch, fear in her gaze. Somehow he'd believed that he was the only screwed up person in the world.

He pushed the image away and rested his head against the back of the rocker so he could gaze up at the ceiling rafters and talk to his wife like he'd talked to her every night since she'd left him. But for the first time since her death, he was stone cold sober.

"Did you see that Gage and Harley brought the twins by today? Laura is pissed at me. I mean, really, *really* pissed. No surprise there. You'd be proud of her, Hannah, really proud at how she stood up against the big bad daddy to protect her sister." A stiff smile worked its way across his mouth. "Lisa…well, she's just like you. Easy to forgive and move on. There were a few tense moments when I thought she'd stand by her sister, but then Jane stepped in and got her to ride Ariel for a few minutes."

Jane. A frown tugged at his brow. She was a puzzle. One moment easy and friendly. The next ready to bolt in fear. "Jane Watts. In case you don't remember her, she's Walter and Barbara's youngest daughter. She's really good with the girls. They both seem to like her a lot. But—"

He paused and mulled over her reaction to his touch, then continued to speak to Hannah as though she were right there in the room with him. "Something bad must have happened to her. All I did was attempt to help her dismount and she froze. Half in, half out of the saddle. At first, I didn't know what to do. Finally I just backed away and gave her space."

He peered up at the ceiling. "Maybe you could, you know, tell her that I'm actually a pretty decent guy? I would never hurt her. I would never hurt any—"

The memory of last spring still haunted him and his voice grew husky. "Harley hugged me today, so I think we'll be okay. But she misses you, baby, and now that she's pregnant, I know she's going to miss you even more."

He listened for the sound of his wife's voice, and wondered if he could only hear her with a belly full of booze. If that was the case, he was definitely going bonkers.

"Baby?" he whispered into the heavy silence, searching the dark rafters for a sign that she was present, the memory of Lisa calling Harley mommy heavy in his heart. "I promise you, I'll do whatever it takes to get our girls back home. And I will never ever let them forget about you, their dear sweet mama."

Then it came, almost like she'd finally heard him, that soft voice in the distance along with a drowsy warmth that enveloped him.

Sleep, honey. Tomorrow's going to be a busy day. Your three girls need you far more than I do.

And he drifted off to sleep knowing full well that Hannah wanted him to help Jane too.

CHAPTER FOURTEEN

The next morning, Jane watched out the window for Mike's truck, her stomach clenched with fear, her heart fluttering like a school girl with a ginormous crush.

After today, she couldn't allow herself to see him again. Her reaction to his attempt to help her down from Pepper had stirred his curiosity. How long before he began to sense that there was something wrong with her, something bad and dirty…

She caught herself before she fell into the dark abyss of the terror filled days and nights she'd lived through, and focused on the fact that she had to continue to hide the worst of it. But she was getting too comfortable around him, beginning to trust him.

And she couldn't do that, or all the ugliness inside of her might escape.

She heard a creak on the basement stairs, then her mother's voice.

"Heading out already?"

"Yes, Mom." She half turned from the window as Barbara came up the staircase. "I'm helping Mike with the girls again today. I left you a note on the table."

"It's a good thing you're doing for that boy." As Barbara reached the porch, she turned and shut the basement door. "What are your plans today?"

"We're picking up Harley and the twins, then taking them to see Sara Coltrane's baby."

"Too bad it's laundry day. I'd love to join you." She crouched down to straighten the boots on the boot rack and when she stood up, sadness elongated her features. "Oh, honey."

It wasn't like her mom to show an unhappy face to anyone but her husband. Jane closed the distance between them and wrapped her arms around the other woman. "What is it, Mom? What's wrong?"

Barbara pressed her face against Jane's shoulder, gripped the sleeves of her jacket, then with a sniffle, released a choked laugh. "It's nothing, honey. I'm just being a silly old goose."

Jane pulled back slightly so she could peer down at her mom's face. "Do you want me to get Dad?"

"Oh God, no." This time she pulled back, dug a tissue out of her pocket, and swiped at the tears. "Forget about me and go have yourself some fun. You deserve to have fun, honey."

Fun. Jane didn't remember how to have fun anymore. For the last few months, there had only been the fear, then the tears, and her mother's comforting presence. It was her turn to step up and help the woman who had so often held her through the darkness of the night. "I am not leaving you alone. I can either call Dad into the house or you can tell me what's bothering you."

Another tear followed the first. "You *do not* want to hear about my troubles, honey. They're selfish and inconsiderate and—"

This had to be big. Her mom was the least selfish, most considerate person she knew. "It's not like you to cry, Mom. Spill, or I'll bug you with the same relentless energy that a five-year-old exhibits on a road trip when asking *are we there yet, are we there yet, are we there yet.*"

Barbara stopped sniffling and regarded her daughter with interest. "Ah, now there's the backbone that's been missing."

"Don't try to turn this on me." With another sniff, Barbara headed into the kitchen. Jane toed off her boots to follow her. "Mom. Talk to me. Well, unless it's about your sex life. If that's the case, you can save the sex talk for Abby."

"Grand babies." Hands on hips, her mother turned, her lavender eyes smoky with guilt. "If you must know, I always thought by now I'd have a grandchild or three to spoil rotten. But it's not going to happen, is it?"

Jane kept her expression neutral. "There's still plenty of time, Mom. Abby is still young enough to—"

"No, *I* was young when I had you children. Barely twenty-two." Barbara crossed to the kitchen doorway where she stopped. Hands on hips, she whirled around to face Jane. "Quite frankly, I'm sick and tired of cooing over other people's grandkids. I want some of my own."

The sound of a vehicle coming up the lane saved her from a heart wrenching conversation about something that would never happen. Jane turned toward the door, and as she zipped up her jacket and tugged on her mitts, she blinked back tears. "Maybe you should go bug Abby then."

Behind her, Barbara sighed. Her clothes rustled as she closed the distance between them and gave Jane a hug from behind. "I'm sorry, honey. I'm just thinking of myself today. Go. Have some fun."

Jane clasped her mom's arms briefly, then pushed out of them before she started sobbing. "Don't hold supper for me. I'm not sure what time I'll be home."

"Okay. Bye, honey."

"See you later, Mom."

Jane shot from the house, letting the screen door bang shut behind her, and hurried through the crisp morning air, thankful for the cold, hoping that Mike would take one look at her red nose and shiny eyes, and put it down to the freezing temperature. She reached the truck, pulled open the door, and climbed into the cab. With a practiced smile, she said, "So day two of winning back the girls."

Mike eyed her, and for a moment, she thought he was going to ask her what was wrong, but then he just nodded, grim. "This is going to take forever, isn't it?"

"Maybe, but they'll come around and then you'll see that it was worth it." He grunted, so she changed the topic. "Nice weather we're having."

He gave a muffled laugh. "Weather. Always a safe topic."

She grinned back, this one more natural than the first. "Want to talk politics instead?"

He slid a glance her way. "Or we could talk about why you're hiding out here."

There it was...the curiosity. She forced what she hoped appeared to be an easy smile. "Or we could talk about Hannah."

With another laugh, he focused on the road. "Weather it is."

And so they chatted easily for the thirty minute drive into town, and when they arrived at Gage's house, he pulled open the door on the very first knock.

Mike's gaze lit up with surprised pleasure when he saw his brother. "Hey bro. Did you call in sick so you could come with us?"

But Gage had a frown on his face and concern in his eyes. "Harley isn't feeling well so I decided to stay home till you picked up the twins. I contacted Abby, and when I told her Jane was going to be with you, she reluctantly agreed." He closed the door behind them. "Girls, your daddy is here."

The twins came down the hallway, quiet and subdued, but when they saw Jane, their relief was palpable.

Laura wrapped her arms around Gage's leg and raised her chin so she could look up at him. "We should stay home and help you take care of Aunt Harley."

He pulled her arms apart and crouched down in front of her, and Jane could see why the girls seemed to love him so much. He was big and tall like his brother. Gentle too. "Your aunt is going to sleep while you're gone. By the time you come home, she'll be ready for you two to entertain her."

While the girls hugged Gage tight, like they'd never let him go, she snuck a peek at Mike. He was watching his brother with the twins, guilt and remorse and gratitude sparking gold flecks in his hazel eyes. As the girls pushed past him and ran outside, he studied his brother. "Are you sure everything's okay with Harley?"

At the mention of his wife's name, Gage's focus turned from the girls back to the hallway. "When she wakes up, I'll take her to the doctor just to make sure." A small grin reshaped his mouth as he turned his gaze back to his brother. "She won't like it, but I'm bigger than she is."

Mike squeezed his brother's shoulder. "We'll call before we bring the girls home, give you a heads up."

"Thanks." His gaze went past them and he pointed out the door. "You might want to get out there before one of them falls out of the back of your truck."

In unison, Mike and Jane turned, and as Mike pushed the door open, he said, "Geez, I'd forgotten how busy they are."

Jane let him go after the girls, and she turned back to the house. "Thank you. Don't worry. They're in good hands."

Without pause, Gage replied, "I know they are. My brother has always been a good person. He was a wonderful husband and father, and he will be one day again."

With a nod and a wave, Jane headed down the sidewalk to help Mike, glad that he had his brother's support.

By the time the girls were strapped in and they were on the road, he initiated a game of *I Spy*, so the trip to the Coltrane ranch passed quickly. Once there, the girls tumbled out of the truck, excited to see the baby.

Laura tugged at Jane's hand, her eyes wide and serious. "Aunt Harley has a baby in her tummy."

She walked beside the tiny girl. "A cousin for you. How exciting."

The older twin nodded. "I get to help feed the baby and change diapers."

Lisa skipped up beside them, dragging Mike by the hand, and wrinkled her nose. "Dirty diapers stink."

Mike grinned down at his youngest daughter. "Not if you love your babies."

Laura gazed up at Jane, her dark eyes shining with innocence, her voice a loud whisper. "Some daddy's hate their kids."

"Oh, sweetie." She glanced at Mike as Lisa tugged him

past them and up the steps to the front door. His jaw was firm, his brows scrunched. Softly she addressed the girl. "Sometimes daddy's make mistakes that they regret."

Laura frowned up at her, but before she could say anything more, the front door opened, revealing a very tired looking cowboy who was in the middle of a big yawn. Nate pushed open the screen door and grumbled, "I've forgotten how often babies need to be fed."

As he backed away to allow them entrance, Jessie slipped up from behind him. She tucked herself against his big body and wrapped her arms around his waist. There were dark circles of exhaustion under her eyes too, and baby spit-up on the shoulder of her t-shirt, but she was happy and smiling. "It's a small price to pay for our precious grandbaby." She waved them all in. "Come in, come in. Sara and Emma just woke from their nap, so this is perfect timing."

As they all scrunched into the tiny boot room, Nate peered outside. "What did you do with Harley?"

Mike bent to unzip Lisa's jacket. "She wasn't feeling well, so she's resting. Gage stayed home from work to keep an eye on her."

"Good. We'll have to call later to see how she's doing." Jessie disengaged from Nate's arms and crouched down to the girls' level, her eyes dancing. "Are you both excited about the baby?"

The twins nodded, and as Lisa opened her mouth to whoop, Mike muffled the sound with one of his hands. He leaned over, his head between the girls, one hand still covering Lisa's mouth, the other on Laura's shoulder. "We have to be quiet so we don't scare Emma. She's not used to loud noises yet."

Lisa pried his hand off her mouth and whispered, "Yes,

Daddy."

Laura shrugged his hand off her shoulder and nodded silently.

After they dispensed with boots and jackets and mitts and toques, Nate veered off into the kitchen while Jessie led the group toward the living room.

Bringing up the rear, Jane watched Mike with the twins. He was big and sweet and gentle, and as he shepherded them ahead of him, she couldn't imagine that the things people said about him were true. But then, if she had to tell anyone what she'd done, no one would believe it either.

Her stomach gave a sick twist, and as they entered the living room where Sara sat on the couch holding her baby daughter, Jane pushed away the memories and leaned one shoulder against the door frame.

The twins tiptoed across the hardwood floor and carefully climbed up on the couch on either side of the new mother, while Mike crouched down in front of her.

Jessie came to a standstill beside Jane, her voice soft and loving. "I could watch them for hours."

She glanced at the other woman's profile. "You don't have to go out on the road for a while, do you?"

"No. I've rearranged my schedule for the next few months." She paused and glanced over at Jane, and there was a sheen of tears in her eyes. "I missed being around when Sara was a baby. There's no way I'm missing this now."

From behind, Nate wrapped his arms around the singer and kissed the top of her head. "Don't mind my wife. Lack of sleep is making her all mushy and weepy."

"Oh honey." With the back of her hands, she wiped the moisture away from her eyes, then put one hand on Jane's arm and changed the subject. "Mike's pretty amazing with the girls, isn't he? It's hard to believe he could hurt anyone."

Nate flatly stated, "That man last spring...that man wasn't Mike."

Jessie clucked her tongue. "Well, it happened. Denying it doesn't make it go away."

And yet, as Jane watched Mike with Sara and the twins, she couldn't help but believe that Nate was right. The man who'd threatened his brother and sister-in-law no longer existed.

The feelings and emotions she'd attempted to ignore filled her heart with something more.

"Would you ladies mind helping me serve the coffee and juice?"

Jane turned her back on the sensation of falling into a deep cavern, and followed her hosts into the kitchen.

Out of sight. Out of mind.

This definitely had to be the last time she allowed herself to be tempted by Mike and his little family.

CHAPTER FIFTEEN

Aware that Jane had stopped somewhere behind him, Mike kept his focus on the twins as they climbed up on the couch next to Sara and Emma. He crouched down in front of them, prepared to intervene should one of the girls get too rambunctious. "How're you doing, kid?"

"I'm exhausted," Sara said with a weary smile as she raised her gaze from the bundle in her arms to his face. "I still can't believe my baby is here. Or that I'm really a mom."

Lisa pressed against her shoulder, craning her neck to get a better view as she attempted to get closer to the baby. "Can I play with your baby?"

Mike reached out, caught her in his arms, and pulled her onto one knee. "Not today, Squirt. Your mommy and I learned really fast that passing you two girls from person to person was a surefire way to upset you."

"All right, Daddy," she said with a disappointed sigh. She leaned into his chest, her legs swinging freely beneath his, and settled in.

Mike raised his gaze to his other daughter and found

Laura watching him, a perplexed expression on her tiny face. But the moment their eyes met, she turned her attention back to the tiny bundle swaddled in the giraffe covered blanket. "Did my daddy help make your baby like he did with my mommy?"

"Wouldn't that freak him out?" With a quiet snort laugh, Sara waggled her dark eyebrows at him before she responded to the older twin. "No, your daddy didn't help make my baby like he did your mommy. That's the easy part." She looked Laura straight in the eyes. "Your daddy helped with the hard part. He stayed with me and held my hand while Emma was being born. I couldn't have done it without him."

Laura peered across at him, something new in her eyes—something that looked a lot like respect and awe. "Really?"

"Really. In fact, even though my parents are going to be Emma's godparents, I want you up with them, Mike. Next to them, I trust you the most with my baby."

Mike's heart filled with love. Then Laura gave him a sweet smile while Lisa reached up and patted his cheek. There was hope for his family. He was certain of it. He just needed to keep his faith that time and love would bring them back together again.

He nodded at Sara. "I'd be honored."

"Great." She shifted forward on the couch. "Since neither Mom nor Dad are here right now to claim holding rights, would you mind? I need a bathroom break." She smiled at the twins. "Would you girls like to see the nursery?"

"*Yes.*"

The twins erupted into motion. Lisa scrambled off his lap. Laura shot off the couch. A couple of minutes later,

Mike held Emma in his arms while Sara ushered the twins out of the living room. There was a flurry of adult chatter, a scramble of approaching feet, and Sara responded with laughter in her voice as she said, "No need to panic. Mike has the baby while I take a bathroom break and show the twins the nursery."

A few seconds later, Jane walked into the room carrying a tray of coffee mugs and juice glasses. She set the tray on the table. "Jessie went with Sara and the twins to the nursery, and Nate headed out to see if his father-in-law wants to join us."

"Sam. That would be great. I haven't seen him since his wife passed away."

"Jessie's mom?" Jane stepped around the coffee table and sat down beside him. Their shoulders touched, but she didn't seem to notice, her attention fixed on the squirming baby in his arms.

"Yeah," he replied as he turned his focus back to Emma. He brushed the back of one finger against her soft cheek, and remembered what it had been like when they'd brought the twins home...exciting and scary and soul-deep right. "Matilda is the reason Jessie and Nate are together today. When she got sick, Nate called Jessie back home. And the rest, they say, is history."

"It's sad that she's gone before she got to see her great-grandchild."

There was an intimacy to this moment that Mike had never shared with anyone but Hannah. He discovered it felt good to have Jane there, her shoulder pressed against his, the light fragrance of whatever she was wearing—for all he knew, it could be Barbara's laundry detergent—filling his head, the gentle expression on her face filled with maternal calmness. And he wondered if this quiet moment together might help her open up.

He cleared his throat. "Having twins makes caring for one baby seem exceptionally easy." He glanced up into her eyes. "What about you? Have you ever thought about having a family?"

She shrugged, the edges of her very kissable mouth turning up as she grinned at him. "Were you eavesdropping on my conversation with my mother this morning?"

Emma gave a wail and squirmed even more. He carefully shifted her onto his shoulder and gently patted her back. "No, but do tell. I'm sure it has something to do with all those baby booties and blankets she knits, then gives away."

She laughed, but then the smile faded as quickly as it had come, and as she turned her gaze back to the newborn, Mike saw a spark of longing in her eyes. "It's true. Apparently my mother would like grandchildren, and she's not happy that neither Abby nor I are co-operating. I'm not ready—I'm not sure that I ever will be—and I don't think my sister is either."

Mike understood. "Hannah wanted a family immediately, but I resisted. We were young, and to be honest, at that point in my life, I wasn't even sure if I ever wanted kids." The baby let out a loud, satisfied belch and immediately settled down again. "But the moment the twins were born, the moment I laid eyes on them, I was hooked. They are the best thing in my life and being a dad is the most important job I can ever have."

"I get that," she said as she once again raised her gaze to his face. "Children learn so much from the way their parents handle things in every day life."

Mike grimaced. "I hope I haven't screwed them up for good."

She laid her hand on his bicep, a reassuring touch that offered hope. "You'll have a few hurdles to get over, but just remember that they need your love most of all."

Before he could respond, his phone vibrated in his shirt pocket, and he pulled it out before it disturbed the baby. He glanced at the screen. "It's Gage."

Jane leaned into his shoulder to see the screen. "Is everything okay?"

As he flashed back to how often Hannah had miscarried, concern unfurled in his belly and spiraled upward to settle in his shoulders. "He's taking Harley to the hospital."

A shuffle of feet at the doorway caught his attention, and Mike saw Laura standing there. Judging by the stricken expression on her face, she'd overheard. A lump formed in his throat.

Mike stood up, the baby asleep against his shoulder, her trust in his care infinite in this big world she'd just entered. Holding Emma gently, he crossed the room so he could crouch down in front of his oldest daughter.

Laura's eyes were huge pools of worry. "Is Aunt Harley going to die like Mommy?"

Mike didn't know what was going on. He didn't want to worry his too serious older daughter, but he also didn't want to lie to her. "Sometimes mommies-to-be get sick and then they need to see the doctor to make sure the baby is healthy."

There was a minuscule relaxation in her body. "Doctor George?"

"No, sweetheart. Doctor George is Aunt Harley's brother, but he'll make sure she has a doctor he can count on to take excellent care of her." He made a decision he hoped he wouldn't regret. "Would you like to go to the hospital so we can find out firsthand? They probably won't let us see Aunt Harley, but maybe we'll be able to talk to Uncle Gage to find out what's going on."

She nodded, silent, her hands folded beneath her chin as she watched him straighten. As Mike turned to hand the baby back to Sara, he realized that everyone in the house had crowded around to listen to the news.

Nate spoke first. "Keep us informed."

He nodded. "As soon as we find out anything, we'll text or call."

Jessie touched his arm. "If there's anything we can do, let us know and we'll be there."

In the flurry of activity that followed—ushering the subdued twins toward the porch, zipping up jackets, putting on boots and mitts and toques—Mike's insides were tight, his gut rolling. But in that short space of time, he realized that each one of them were there for the other.

They were community.

No, they were more than that. They were family…and it had been wrong of Hannah to demand he keep her illness a secret. Maybe if they'd allowed the people who loved them into their life and problems, they would have had the emotional support they needed to get through the tough times.

Hannah would still have died, but Mike would have had the support to keep him sane, and maybe he wouldn't have screwed up so badly with Harley and the twins.

Nate pulled on his winter coat and boots and followed them out to the truck where Laura and Lisa quickly scrambled up into the back seat. "Remember to call if they need anything and to let us know how Harley's doing."

As Mike buckled Laura in and Jane buckled Lisa in, they said their goodbyes. Then he climbed into the truck and with a wave, pointed the truck toward town.

It was different than his last trip to town. There was more on the line this time. It was no longer just about him regaining custody of his daughters. This time it was all about Harley.

Because if Harley lost the baby...well, her and Gage would mourn the loss, then get on with the business of making another baby, just like Hannah and Mike had done.

But if the twins lost their Aunt Harley...he turned his thoughts from there and focused on the long drive into town, a heavy silence overriding everything else.

At the hospital, Laura chewed on her bottom lip with worry, and walked at his side. Mike wished he could lift her into his arms and hold her close and comfort her. But the mere fact that she held tightly onto his hand spoke volumes about how scared she was.

Inside the hospital, they headed to the front desk where Mike told them who they were and who they wanted to see. The receptionist glanced at her notes and shook her head. "She's resting right now."

Mike saw the disappointment on his daughters' faces, saw the glint of tears in Laura's eyes, and said, "It's important. I have two little girls here who are scared to death. They need to see that their aunt is okay."

The nurse stood up to peer over the desk at them, then reluctantly nodded. She shook her finger at the twins. "No noise or I'll kick you out myself."

"Thank you." Mike crouched down in front of them. "We have to be very quiet. Tiptoe quiet. Aunt Harley is resting and we don't want to disturb her."

Lisa nodded, then silently zipped her mouth shut and threw away the key.

Mike continued, gently preparing them. "Even if she's

awake, Aunt Harley might not be able to hug you. No climbing on her. We don't want to hurt her tummy or the baby."

"Yes, Daddy," Laura nodded earnestly.

When he stood up, Jane was gazing at him with tears in her eyes and something else. Something that looked a lot like affection. He didn't quite know what to do with that. He was attracted to her, without question, but it was obvious she wasn't interested in that kind of relationship.

And even if she was, he'd be betraying Hannah...

Pushing away the thought, he focused on the next few minutes. As they proceeded, the girls tiptoeing with each step they made, Laura held Mike's hand, and Lisa clung on to Jane's. And when they reached the room and stopped in the doorway, he saw that Harley had her eyes closed.

Beside the bed sat a very somber Gage gently holding her hand.

They must have made a noise because Gage suddenly lifted his head and pushed to his feet, releasing his wife's hand to come to the door.

Mike squeezed him on the shoulder, his voice barely above a whisper. "The twins wanted to see Harley."

His brother glanced down at the girls. "Understandable."

Harley's voice drifted from behind him. "Is that Laura and Lisa?"

Gage partially turned, still blocking the doorway. "Yes. If you're too tired, they can come back later."

Her pale hand lifted from the bed and she beckoned them forward. "Come closer, girls. I've missed you."

Without missing a beat, Gage crouched down in front of the twins. "No climbing on the bed. You can hold her hand only."

"Yes, Unca Gage," they whispered in unison.

He stepped aside and let them pass, and when he saw that they were being careful, he pulled Mike and Jane into the hallway out of earshot, careful to keep his wife within view.

"It's the baby," he said, and suddenly he had tears in his eyes.

Mike could relate. Hannah's three miscarriages had been heartbreaking. He put his hand on his brother's shoulder. "I'm sorry. George will make sure that everything is done to take good care of both of them."

"I know."

Jane squeezed his arm. "Nate and Jessie said that if there's anything they can do, just call." She exchanged a look with Mike. "Us too, anything at all."

"Thanks," Gage murmured. He rubbed the back of his neck and eyed his brother. "I need you to take the twins home for the night."

Surprised, Mike nodded. "Of course. I'll call Abby and let her know that I've got them."

And as they followed Gage back in, Mike wondered if Abby would even allow that, or would she sweep in and take the twins away from him.

Gage sat down on the chair next to the bed and gathered the girls on his lap. "Your aunt has to stay here until the doctor says it's okay for her to go home, and I'm staying with her. So you're going to have to be brave and go with your daddy. He loves you and wants to take care of you."

Laura began to chew on her bottom lip again. Lisa started to squirm. Gage glanced up at Jane. "Maybe Jane can stay and help. You like Jane, don't you?"

"Thanks, bro," Mike muttered. "Nothing like putting her on the spot."

Ignoring him, Jane smiled down at the girls. "Of course they like me. They *adore* me. We'll do our hair, and maybe we'll even paint your daddy's fingernails pink."

The twins muffled their giggles in their hands. Mike crossed the room and kissed Harley on the cheek. "Take care, sister-in-law. Watch out that this big lug gets some sleep."

She smiled weakly, her exhaustion apparent. "I will."

Then Mike hugged Gage. "Call me with any news."

And then they were walking out of the hospital, climbing into the truck, the twins craning their head to look at the hospital as they drove away.

They stopped at Gage's house to pick up a few things for the twins, then at the Watts ranch so Jane could grab an overnight bag and let her parents know what was going on. Barbara looked twitchy and worried, which surprised Mike. Maybe she didn't trust him as much as she said he did. He frowned at her. "Is there something you want to say to me?"

Barbara exchanged a look with Walter, then with her daughter. "No."

Then they were driving the last few miles home, and while this wasn't the way he would have planned the girls' return, the mere fact that they were staying with him boosted his conviction that everything would work out and they'd soon be a family again.

But after a painfully quiet supper, an unusually somber bath time, and bedtime without a single objection, Mike was pretty sure he wouldn't sleep a wink…not with two of the saddest little girls he'd seen under his roof in forever.

Of course, that wasn't even taking into consideration the one very nervous woman who, as daylight had faded into darkness and the door lock deadbolts were clicked into place, looked like she might expire from the sheer terror of being locked into the house with him and the girls.

CHAPTER SIXTEEN

It was damp, dark, cold. And she was naked, her wrists chained to the post in the middle of the container. Her teeth rattled together, and it wasn't just the dropping temperatures.

He was on his way again.

She'd heard him drive up on his quad a little while ago, and open the door to one of the other containers—there were six in all, she'd counted them that first night—and after a muffled scream of fear, there'd been nothing.

Only the sound of her own harsh breaths sawing in and out of her lungs as she crouched like a wild animal, chained, unable to escape the man who had tricked her into trusting him.

Then she heard the screech of the container door closing, the crunch of gravel beneath his boots as he approached.

A scream clawed up her throat until she could no longer contain it...

Until it forced her to open her mouth and release it...

~~~~~

Jane opened her eyes, momentarily blinded by the ceiling light, disorientated and clawing at the shadow of the man above her, the rational part of her brain wondering…who was that crazy woman screaming and why wouldn't she stop, while the rest of her screamed and sobbed and begged until her throat felt raw.

Then a familiar voice reached through the terror filled nightmare.

"Jane. Wake up, Jane. You're having a bad dream."

Like a lifeline, she recognized Mike's voice and without thought, launched herself full body against him, hanging on to his big body like she'd clung to the cop who had rescued her all those months ago.

"Hush, sweetheart, it's just a nightmare. You're here with me. Safe."

His soft voice washed over her and she held on tighter for fear he'd vanish in a fog of hallucination. He had his arms wrapped around her, holding her close, rocking her like a mother might rock a small child. Like Sara rocked Emma.

A wee bit more of the fear fell away.

But she refused to let go, her face pressed into the spot at the junction of his neck and shoulder. She inhaled the clean familiar scent of him, felt his words rumble from his chest into hers, slowing her heart rate marginally, steadying her nerves until she was finally brave enough to open her eyes again.

What she saw made her sag against the man holding her up.

She was in Mike's spare bedroom. There on the dresser were the clean clothes she'd set out for tomorrow, her hairbrush on top of them, her backpack with the rest of her items on the chair next to the dresser.

Nothing put away. So she could run the moment things turned sideways.

Then she spotted the wide-eyed girls. They stood in the open doorway holding hands, their pink and white flannel sleepwear dotted with tiny lime green hearts, Laura with a teddy bear in one arm, Lisa sucking hard on the thumb in her mouth...and Jane was suddenly, totally back in the present.

Present and accounted for.

She pushed out of the refuge of Mike's arms, scrubbed at her wet face, and whispered, "The girls."

But the man in the soft white t-shirt, worn jeans, and bare feet wasn't letting go. Keeping a secure hold on her hand—she knew what he was trying to do, ground her to the present and him—he turned to the twins and beckoned them forward. "Come here."

They raced forward into his outstretched arm, and he gathered them close so they could climb up, one on his lap, the other on the bed beside Jane.

She sat back against the headboard and forced a smile. "I'm sorry I woke you."

Laura reached up and brushed away the hair that had stuck to Jane's sweaty forehead, her sweet face concerned. "Did you have a bad dream?"

Jane nodded, trying to be brave for the twins, wishing she could climb onto Mike's lap like the younger twin.

Lisa pulled her thumb out of her mouth. "We have bad dreams sometimes too." She held her thumb out. "Want some? It helps vanquish the boogey man."

A bit more of her tension eased and she held her thumb out. "Thank you. I have one of my own, if I need it."

Laura giggled and laid her head against Jane's shoulder, then gave her a one armed hug around the waist. "Silly

Jane. Grownups don't suck on their thumb."

Mike ruffled his oldest daughter's sleep-tangled hair, then pulled Lisa's arm down before her thumb ended back into her mouth. "Maybe we do and that's why we don't want you sucking your thumb now. You'll wear it out before you really need it."

Lisa stretched out her arms and patted his face between her hands. "Silly daddy."

He smiled down at his youngest daughter, then raised his gaze to Jane's face. There was so much concern in his kind eyes, it broke her heart. He had the girls to worry about. He didn't need to worry about her too.

She discreetly tried to pull her hand away, but he wasn't letting go, and she finally relented. Not because she needed him there—she could sleep with her eyes open and the lights on all by herself, thank you very much—but because she liked the feel of his warm hand clasping her cold one.

Laura held her teddy bear in front of Jane's face, blocking her view of the hunky man with the chiseled jaw and rock hard abs. "Here, you can have Ralph so that you won't be lonely."

Jane smiled at the twin and shook her head. "Thank you, but I couldn't."

"I insist." The five-year-old tucked the bear into the crook of Jane's neck. "Besides, I have Lisa to keep me company so I'm never really alone."

Jane patted the bear's back. "Thank you so very much."

Mike finally released Jane's hand, his focus on the twins. "Now that you know Jane is okay, do you think you can go back to sleep?"

Lisa yawned and nodding her head, laid it against her dad's shoulder.

Laura climbed onto her knees, kissed Jane on the cheek, then kissed the teddy bear and climbed off the bed.

Mike didn't push off the bed immediately. Instead, he rearranged his youngest daughter against his front monkey-style, then grabbed Laura by the arm and tugged her up on the bed behind him so she straddled his back. As she wrapped her arms around his neck, his gaze remained steady on Jane. "I'll tuck in the girls and be right back. I won't be gone longer than a few minutes, okay?"

The thought of being left alone sent her heart back into panic mode, but she bravely forced a breezy tone into her voice, and held up the bear. "I'm fine, really. Besides, I have Ralph."

His expression remained concerned. "I'll be right back. Don't go anywhere."

As she watched the big man push to his feet and carry the twins out, she wondered where he thought she might go. It wasn't like she had a vehicle…or a way to escape…

She clasped her knees to her chest, Ralph pressed between her chest and thighs, and listened to the deep soothing sound of Mike's voice, the giggles of the twins, and she began the process of gathering her defenses around her so that when he came back in, she could convince him she was fine.

It had been a couple of months since she'd had a nightmare. She thought she was getting better, but maybe she never would.

She scraped her hands through her hair, her fingers trembling, her stomach clenched in panic at the thought of being alone in the dark.

Maybe she should get up and watch TV till morning. She'd keep the volume way down or she'd be sure to have a visitor or two—

Then Mike reentered the room, his large presence sucking the air from her lungs. The white t-shirt clung to his upper body like it was one size too small, revealing wide shoulders, six pack abs, and a body worth clinging to.

For the first time since she'd been rescued, desire hit her, hot and heavy and delicious. It flushed her body and awakened body parts that she'd been certain were dead.

As she watched him approach, trepidation warred with desire. Instead of tucking her in and leaving, he climbed onto the bed, put an arm around her shoulders, and drew her against his hard chest.

Jane rested her head against his shoulder and placed her palm over his heart so she could feel the steady beat. It soothed her further, and as she inhaled the scent of him, she began to feel restless and itchy.

His voice rumbled in his chest. "Want to tell me about your nightmare?"

"Oh God no," she breathed, snuggling closer to the warmth of him. She felt—*safe*—with him there.

Her hand inched up his chest till it rested on the back of his neck, and when she raised her chin so she could look up at him, he shifted and tilted his head to look down at her. And suddenly, unexpectedly, they were almost mouth to mouth.

The urge to kiss him felt so right, Jane went with it, raising her head from his shoulder, pulling his head down to meet her halfway. And as their lips touched, an explosion of desire rocked her body and set her off like a wild thing.

CHAPTER SEVENTEEN

Without thought, Mike dove into the kiss.

Her lips were warm and pliable beneath his, and his body took over before his brain could make sense of what they were doing, where it could lead.

Because right this very moment, there was only Jane and him and this desire between them.

He put his other arm around her shoulders, clasping her to him and she reacted like a wild desperate thing, climbing onto him, straddling his lap, tugging her nightgown out of the space between them and rocking against him with a keening keel that shot an arrow right to the center of his own need.

But he didn't want the first time with her to be over in eight seconds or less, and with a muffled laugh against her mouth, he grabbed her by the upper arms and said, "Whoa, honey, slow down."

And just like that, everything between them changed.

She was whimpering now, sounds of fear instead of desire, and she fought his hold on her like his hands were iron-clad shackles. Mike saw the fear in the glaze of her eyes. He released her, then had to capture her by the wrists before she could claw at his face.

"Jane, it's me, Mike," he said, giving her a small shake with hopes that he could nudge her back to reality before she went off the deep end and never came back.

She froze.

The deep purple hues of her irises cleared and he recognized the moment their position on the bed registered in her brain. Scrambling away from him, she tumbled off the bed and landed on the hardwood floor with a surprised *oomph*, revealing her long bare legs and damp panties...

He forced his gaze back to her face and stayed right where he was, afraid if he moved he might set her off again. "It's okay, Jane. You're okay." He kept talking, even if it half sounded like nonsense. "Well, I think you're okay. It's not like I'm coming over there to find out. Although that was a pretty hard fall. *Are* you okay?"

She blinked up at him, the fear and confusion tempered by the bright lights. He forced himself to remain still and calm and relaxed.

A non-threat.

Although what he'd like to do right now was rip off the head of whoever had done this to her.

Keep talking, he reminded himself and he casually raised one brow. "Isn't it kind of cold down there?"

She blinked again, and peered around as though sorting out where she was. When she finally scrambled to her feet and stood at the edge of the bed, he slowly rolled over to the opposite side and onto his feet.

He'd landed on the side of the bed with the door to his back and he could clearly see in her expressive eyes the second she realized that she was trapped.

That she'd have to go through him to escape.

Surprising him, she held her ground, teeth bared like a wild animal about to jump into the fray. "Get out of my way."

Mike stepped aside, giving her plenty of room to skirt around him. "I'm not going to stop you from leaving, Jane."

She stood there, her gaze skittering back and forth between him and the door, but she didn't move.

He was no psychologist, but he knew real fear when he saw it. "What happened to you?"

Her lips thin, the paleness of her face replaced by a flush of her cheeks, she dropped her gaze to the floor.

"Nothing," she muttered.

Someone had hurt her and hurt her bad. He wondered if that's where the scar on her lip had come from.

Mike forced himself to remain outwardly calm, his hands relaxed at his sides, while his rage inside threatened to boil over. "I'm not going to hurt you."

Jaw clenched, cheeks flushed, she looked him square in the eyes. "Despite what it looks like right now, I'm not afraid of you."

"Good, because I'm freaking terrified of you." He blew out a breath, and raking his hands through his hair, he stalked toward the door. Before he went through, he stopped. "When you're ready to tell me the truth, I'll be here. No judgment. Only understanding."

Mike left her alone and headed down the hallway to the family room where he'd set up a bed on the couch because he hadn't been able to bear the thought of sleeping in the master bedroom without his wife. But now—as he plunked down on the couch and scraped a hand across his face—he mulled over the fact that he hadn't thought about Hannah once. Not while he was holding Jane in his arms, comforting her. Not while he was invested in their kiss.

Betrayal settled heavy in his gut.

He'd fallen for Jane. How could he so soon after his wife's death? What kind of person did that make him? It wasn't that he was out of love with Hannah. It was just that Jane, with her dark secretive eyes and ready laughter, with her kindness and hidden strength, had wormed herself into his heart too.

Was his heart big enough for them both?

He glanced at the doorway and resisted the urge to retrace his steps down the hallway to ensure she was okay, then remembered her kiss and how she'd pressed her body against his.

For a moment, he'd found heaven on earth again.

With an exhausted sigh, knowing full well he'd have to get up in a few short hours, he flipped on the TV and muted the sound.

There was only one path left for him to follow…help the frightened woman in his house heal and pray they both came out of this with their hearts intact.

CHAPTER EIGHTEEN

Jane woke to the sound of sizzling bacon, the rich smoky scent filling her nostrils, and her stomach growled. For the first time in forever, she was hungry...really hungry.

As she rolled out of bed and her feet touched the cold hardwood floor, the memory of last night rolled over her like a summer breeze.

Kissing Mike had been cathartic, almost the best therapy in the world. She'd wanted him, desired him, and for a few seconds she'd forgotten everything else. The dream, her fear, the fact that she was dirty inside and out.

Her good mood deflated, and she crawled back under the covers, too humiliated to leave the room.

Mike must have thought she was certifiably nuts, climbing all over him like a sex starved woman, then shrieking like she'd been inflicted with the crazies.

Even though the psychiatrist she'd gone to see had told her that if she did the work, she could eventually be a normal woman again, Jane hadn't believed her, and her reaction last night proved the improbability of ever having a relationship with a man again.

Which was really sad.

She'd never again experience the high of making love with a man who touched her soul, never again experience the sweet aftermath of waking in a lover's arms, safe, protected, adored.

Nor would she ever be able to give her mom the grandchildren she so desperately wanted.

The best that she could hope for was a life filled with wanting what she was too afraid to welcome into her life.

But she couldn't stay under the covers forever, hiding her shame, so she climbed out of bed and dressed, stopping in the bathroom only long enough to take care of the necessities. Then she tiptoed to the bedroom door, opened it slightly to peer down the hallway—

She could hear Mike's deep tones, and Lisa answered him in her beautiful singsong voice while Laura, it seemed, was back to judging him silently.

She'd vowed to help out and despite her utter embarrassment from last night, she'd do just that. Maybe he'd keep his distance, which would be a pity because she'd enjoyed the press of her body into his...

Jane dragged her thoughts from that path, and venturing out of the bedroom, headed to the kitchen. As she passed the other bedrooms, she saw the twins' beds were unmade and the master bedroom untouched. She wondered where Mike had slept, and then she saw the pillow and neatly folded blanket on the arm of the couch in the family room.

The man had lost his wife and was still grieving for her, and she had *kissed* him. No doubt he'd be as eager to avoid her as she was him.

In the kitchen entrance she silently observed Mike pulling bacon out of the pan, the girls at the table, Lisa madly scribbling across pages of the coloring book, deliberately staying outside the lines like it was some badge of honor—*the little rebel*—while Laura stared intently at the book in her hands, her mouth moving as she silently read the words.

An early reader. Jane liked that.

And then almost as if he'd sensed her, Mike turned from the stove. Their eyes connected and her heart fluttered in her throat while her cheeks turned warm and her legs turn to jelly.

His slow sexy drawl turned her panties indecently wet.

"Look who finally crawled out of bed, girls." He turned back to the stove and cracked an egg into the pan. "You're just in time for breakfast, Jane."

Lisa jumped off the chair and ran toward her, the thump of her feet making the dishes in the china cabinet rattle. "*Jane, Jane*, want to help me color?"

As the five-year-old skidded to a stop in front of her, Jane ruffled the girl's tangled hair. "I should help your daddy with breakfast."

"No need. I've got it under control." Pulling open the fridge, Mike lifted out a bowl of sliced fruit and carried it to the table. Then he pulled out a chair, his gaze holding her hostage. "Sit. I'll bring you coffee."

She blushed and lowered her eyes as she obeyed him. "You don't have to wait on me."

Silent behind her, he tucked in her chair like a gentleman. He didn't touch her, didn't even smell her hair like a man smitten, which was rather disappointing. She reminded herself that he loved his wife very much. And the fact that he kissed her back when she'd attacked him…well, even though he lost his wife six months ago, he was still a man with physical needs.

"Thank you," she murmured, and she couldn't help but

watch him walk back to the stove. Tall, broad shouldered, hard all over.

Simply delicious.

Laura's voice rang out, accusing. "Why are you looking at my daddy all gooey-eyed?"

Jane blushed and focused on the twin. "Sorry. I'm just very thankful for his kindness."

Mouth thin, Laura glared at her before she returned her attention to the book, and Jane made a silent vow to keep her focus off the hot man cooking breakfast.

The table had already been set. Peanut butter and jam to go with the toast. Salt and pepper for the eggs. A bowl filled to the top with freshly cut slices of oranges, pineapple, pears, and apples. There was a place setting for everyone, but the head of the table was empty.

Hannah's place, she guessed, and made a mental note to avoid the spot.

Then Mike carried plates of bacon and eggs to the table. "Books and crayons away, monkeys. Breakfast is here."

The girls quickly obeyed, appetites clearly at the ready, and when all the plates were delivered and Mike sat down, he bowed his head and said a simple prayer. "God bless this food, this house, and everyone in it. Amen."

In unison, Jane and the twins murmured, "Amen."

Then the girls gobbled their breakfast like they hadn't eaten in days. Mike grinned at Jane. "They inherited their mother's looks and my appetite."

Laura slowed down, one eye on her daddy, suspicion and distrust filling her gaze. "Don't talk about Mommy," she said around a mouthful of food, and Mike stared back at her, his face void of expression.

Now that the initial embarrassment was over and Jane was certain Mike wasn't going to bring up the way she'd

attacked him last night—at least not in front of the twins—
she focused on the day. "So what's the plan today?"

Laura paused, fork halfway to her mouth. "Can we see
Aunt Harley?"

Compassion colored the cowboy daddy's expression.
"How about if we start with calling Uncle Gage to see if
it's okay?"

Her expression crumbled, and she ducked her head and
nodded.

Mike lifted his hand to touch her, then obviously
thought better of it.

Feeling their pain, Jane's shoulders slumped. "Sweetie,
your aunt needs her rest right now, but as soon as the
doctor says she can have visitors, we'll take you to see
her."

Lisa piped up, "And Unca Gage."

Looking relieved, Mike responded. "You bet. They love
you girls lots, like I do."

Laura's mouth thinned. She pushed away her empty
plate and crossed her arms over her chest. "May I be
excused?"

"*Please* be excused. And yes, you may," Mike replied
easily. As he set down his fork and knife beside his plate,
he watched his oldest daughter stomp to the sink with her
dishes, and Jane recognized the concerned expression on
his face. "If we have some time before we see your uncle
and aunt, would you like to take a ride on your ponies?"

Lisa started woofing down her food while Laura set her
dishes in the sink, then turned to eye him with suspicion.
"Is Jane coming?"

Jane straightened on her chair, and gave the girl a bright
smile. "Of course. I'll do up the dishes first, then follow
you."

With a belligerence that was reminiscent of a teen, Laura crossed her arms over her chest and glared at her dad. "When are you going to call Uncle Gage?"

Mike turned his attention to the food on his plate, and picked up his knife and fork. "As soon as I'm finished eating. You can brush your teeth while you're waiting."

Lisa jumped down from the chair, grabbed her empty plate, raced around the table, and dropped the plate and silverware into the sink. Jane winced at the clatter and hoped nothing was broken. As the younger twin raced from the room, Laura following at a much slower pace, Mike pushed away his half eaten plate of food. "I have a lot to make up for, don't I?"

Without thinking, Jane covered his hand with hers. "They need time to adjust."

He captured her hand, rubbing the back with his thumb, sending tiny tingles up her arm, then raised his gaze to her face, his voice quiet and serious. "I enjoyed kissing you last night."

So he'd brought it up, as though it were on his mind too. Jane's cheeks heated, and tugging her hand out of his, breaking physical contact, she dropped her gaze to her plate. "I'm sorry about last night. I don't know what came over me."

In her peripheral vision, she could see Mike push back his chair, and pick up his plate and her own. "No need to apologize. Just know that if you ever need to talk to someone, Jane, I'm here and I'm a good listener."

As he went to the sink and turned on the faucet, she pushed away from the table, cleared off the remaining dishes, and grabbed the tea towel to dry. Compatible silence settled between them while the radio played softly in the background and the twins' giggles drifted down the hallway.

An angry scream erupted from the bathroom and she set aside the towel. "I'll go see what they're up to."

Jane took a single step away, then turned back and placed one hand on the hard muscles of his back. He stilled, and the warmth of his body seeped into her palm and fingers. "You're a good man, Mike Toryn. A good daddy too. Don't let anyone tell you otherwise."

Before he could say anything in response, she walked away, following the childish giggles into the bathroom where she found the girls with toothpaste in their hair.

And as she helped them wash out the gooey mess, she decided to enjoy each moment with this tiny family...because soon they wouldn't want her around.

CHAPTER NINETEEN

Mike headed to the stables with an excited Lisa skipping and giggling and talking nonstop about what she planned to do with her pony. She had her hand tucked into his, and he could feel the warmth of her fingers through the wool mittens she wore.

"I remember how to brush Ariel, Daddy. Remember that we like to gallop? It's better to gallop in the summer though." She paused to take a breath, and craned her neck to look up at him. "How long is it till summer?"

"About six months." He grinned down at her. She was a chatterbox and busy bee, but she also had an open disposition that allowed her to forgive easily and be happy naturally. Whereas Laura...

The older twin was suspicious of everything and everyone, and didn't forgive or forget easily. It would be a challenge to win her over—and where Laura went, Lisa would follow. But he was in this for the long haul, so it didn't matter how long it took, he'd have patience.

Lisa suddenly tugged her hand free and raced ahead toward the horse barn, grabbing the door handle with both hands. She gave a tug, but the heavy door wouldn't budge.

"Daddy, hurry up," she demanded. "Daddy, I want to see Ariel *now*."

Mike quickened his step. "I'm coming, squirt."

Together they pulled the door open and she raced ahead, down the aisle, straight to Ariel's stall where she wiggled her way through an opening in the gate so she could hug her pony.

Mike wasn't concerned. The pony was gentle and extremely tolerant of small children. "I'll get the brushes, Lisa. Stay right there."

As he collected the items he needed from the tack room and placed them into a bucket, he caught a glimpse of Laura tugging Jane out of the house. Relief washed over him. The older twin might be unwilling to show it, but it appeared that when he wasn't around to see, she was happy to be back home in familiar surroundings.

He turned his attention to the woman being dragged along in his daughter's wake. She was laughing and easy with the twin, and he hoped it would last till they got to the barn and beyond.

Because the desire to get to know her better continued to grow.

The memory of their kiss sent a pulse of desire south of his belt, forcing him to take a deep breath to prepare for their next encounter. He vowed to be casual—no going in for another kiss while she was in mid-sentence. It might permanently scare her away.

The woman was skittish one moment and wilding responsive the next. He wanted her to relax so he could get to know her better, except getting to know her better felt…wrong. And because of that, there was a lodge of guilt in his belly and confusion in his brain.

How could he be falling for another woman so soon after the loss of his wife?

He'd loved Hannah so very much, but she was gone. And Jane was right here, and the woman teasing him with thoughts of the future was funny and sexy and terrific with his daughters.

Maybe all he had to do was avoid being alone with her. And not kiss her.

And keep his hands off her.

Especially keep his hands off her because it seemed that every time he touched her, she froze right up.

There were moments when she forgot herself and responded though, like last night when they'd been in her bed together. He hoped she'd eventually talk to him because he couldn't help her if he didn't know what had caused her nightmare.

Bucket in hand, still mulling over the tight-lipped woman who fascinated him, Mike turned from the window and headed out of the tack room. But when he crossed the straw covered aisle to Ariel's stall, a feeling of unease churned in his belly. He tugged open the gate and panic hit him square in the gut.

"Lisa," he shouted and heard her giggle from overhead. He looked up and found her standing on the loft overlooking the bullpen.

Mike dropped the bucket, noting that the ladder to the upper level was still up, barricading the stairs.

"How did you get up there, monkey?" he asked as he pulled down the ladder and started to climb up after her. But she wasn't listening, and when she began to jump up and down, he had a vision of her losing her footing and falling into the bullpen.

"Daddy, Daddy. Cyclone is *humongous*."

169

"Yes, he is," he said, making his way over to her, quiet and steady so as not to excite her or the now thrashing bull in the pen. "Lisa, honey, stop jumping. Cyclone doesn't like the noise or the excitement."

She did as he asked and peered over the edge, dangerously close to tipping over. One wrong move and she could be in the bullpen, trampled to death in a millisecond. "Cyclone looks mad."

"Yeah, he's not the only one," Mike muttered, checking his temper, aware of Jane and Laura entering the barn and coming to a halt near Ariel's stall. He made his way across the timbers until he reached his youngest daughter, and when he finally did—when he had an arm secure around her waist so if she did lose her balance she wouldn't tumble in—the tight band around his chest eased.

"I've got her," he called out so Jane and Laura would know she was okay. Then he narrowed his focus on the troublemaker. "Did you forget my rule about Cyclone?"

She twisted in his arms so she faced him directly, and her big sad eyes and the disappointed droop of her mouth nearly did him in. "No Daddy, but I missed him so much."

Mike's heart cracked. But he had to keep her safe and make her understand. "Cyclone has one objective in his life and that's to hurt anyone who comes near him. So you have to stay away from him, Lisa."

Her lower lip protruded and she slid a glance toward the bullpen. "Cyclone and me are besties. He would never hurt me."

Mike took a deep breath and lowered his voice. "Lisa, Cyclone is capable of killing you. Do you know how your sister would feel if she lost you?"

Lisa tipped to the side, clearly confident that he would hang on to her, and peered around his shoulder at her sister.

"She'd be gigantically sad."

Mike nodded and for emphasis added, "Sadder than when she lost Mommy."

Straightening, his youngest daughter threw her arms around his neck and pressed her face into the crook of his shoulder. "I won't make Laura sad, I promise, Daddy."

He picked her up into his arms, safe and unhurt, and carried her across the rafters to the ladder. Once they were back on the main floor, Lisa ran to Laura and hugged her, and Laura hugged her back.

Jane came to stand beside him, nudging his shoulder with her own. "That was some pretty sweet talking, cowboy."

"She scared the hell out of me," he breathed, his heart suddenly pumping as the adrenaline kicked in.

Throwing her arms around his waist for a quick hug, she said, "I'm sure it won't be the last time."

Then Lisa ran up to them, dragging her sister behind. "Daddy, can we go see Mommy now?"

A very annoyed Laura kicked her sister in the shin. "She means Aunt Harley."

"Can we? Can we? Can we?" Lisa jumped up and down, the incident with Cyclone apparently forgotten as though it had never happened.

Mike made a mental note to keep her in his sights at all times. "Let me call your uncle and see if it's okay."

As Lisa twirled away, no doubt already onto mischief plan B or C or Z, Laura stared up at him, impatient while he pulled out his cell to place the call, her hands folded under her chin, concern in her eyes.

The call went to voice mail. Mike tried to give her a reassuring smile, but he was worried too. "Hey bro. We're all wondering how Harley is feeling today. Give me a call when you get this message."

Mike hit disconnect, then tucked the phone back into his pocket and crouched down in front of Laura. "Let's go brush Belle. It'll make the time go faster until Uncle Gage calls back."

She nodded, quiet, and his too serious daughter picked up the big bucket and lugged it to the stalls while Jane chased Lisa down the aisle.

A few minutes later, his phone rang. Laura ducked under Belle's neck, her intense gaze fixed on him while he answered the call. He beckoned her forward, crouched down, and put the device on speaker. "Hey bro, I have one very worried daughter here. How's Harley doing?"

"Sorry, Mike. I had my phone off while she was sleeping. She's feeling better and would love to see the girls."

Laura put one arm around Mike's shoulders to balance herself as she leaned forward. "Uncle Gage, can we come now?"

"Hey Sugarplum," Gage drawled, and Mike could feel Laura's tiny body relax against his own. It felt good to have her close, but he was certain it wouldn't last. "How about if you bring your sister and Daddy and Jane by this afternoon? That way we can have a good long visit."

"Visit?" she asked. She shoved away from Mike, her eyes getting all squinty and suspicious. "Can't we come back home to live with you and Aunt Harley?"

Home. Mike wanted to remind her that this was her home, but he knew he hadn't earned that right yet. So he held the cell steady in the palm of his hand and asked, "What's the status on that?"

There was a moment of silence before Gage replied. "A few days. Maybe a couple of weeks. The doctor wants

172

Harley on complete bed rest until he says otherwise."

Lisa skidded to a stop in front of the phone and leaned in so close, her mouth was almost pressing against the device. "We miss you, Unca Gage."

"We miss you and your sister too, Sugarpie." In the background, there was a tinkle of a bell. "Your aunt is calling me, so I gotta go. See you all after lunch."

Mike saw the call had been disconnected, so he tucked the cell back into his shirt pocket and eyed his oldest daughter. "I guess we should make arrangements for the bus to pick you up here for the next week or two."

She kicked at the straw covered floor. "I s'pose."

"Well then." He pushed to his feet, noticed both Lisa and Jane were staring at the dejected girl in front of him, and wondered what they should do. They still had three hours to kill until lunchtime. He took a deep breath and exhaled noisily, drawing Laura's attention off her pink snow boots. "I guess all we can do for now is finish the work we started, then go get cleaned up and have some lunch before we head into town."

Laura nodded and turned and reentered Belle's stall.

Lisa tucked her hand into his, drawing his attention. "It's okay, Daddy. Laura just likes to be grumpy sometimes, but she'll get over it when she sees Uncle Gage and Mommy."

Then with a grin up at him, she slipped her hand free and skipped away to help her sister brush down Belle.

Mike glanced over at Jane. "What about you? Do you have time to stick around for a week or two?"

She smiled softly, the kind of smile that stopped his heart, then sent it galloping off into the sunset. "You bet. This is a golden opportunity to prove to Abby that you're capable of taking care of the girls."

He was definitely in trouble here. Not only did he have
one daughter who hated him and another who was a born
risk taker, but now he had a woman who tempted him to
look to the future.

*Hannah, will you hate me if I fall all the way in love
with her?*

When he didn't get an answer right away, he shook off
the heavy mantle of despair, grabbed Jane by the hand, and
dragged her over to join the girls.

Soon he was surrounded by three laughing and giggling
females. And when Jane raised her gaze, her laughter
turned to a silent question.

"What?" she mouthed, and he smiled and swooped in,
scooping Jane into his arms for a spin, then letting her go
so he could capture the twins and give them a whirly spin,
which caused eardrum shattering screams followed by
joyful childish laughter.

The temporary deafness was totally worth it.

When he put the girls down, he said, "Last one to the
house has to make lunch."

And the four of them raced out of the barn.

As Mike deliberately trailed behind them, the frosty
temperature in the air biting at his cheeks, he realized that
he couldn't remember the last time he was this happy.

For the first time since he buried his beautiful wife,
there was hope in his heart and love in the air.

CHAPTER TWENTY

A few days later, it stormed. One of those can't-see-past-your-nose, wind whipping the flakes past the window kind of snowfalls.

Jane moved about the kitchen preparing supper while Mike entertained the twins in the living room. They were laughing and giggling and having fun, and her heart released a happy sigh.

In the past week, everyone had fallen into a routine.

Mike was the first up, waking the girls to catch the bus, and by the time Jane climbed out of bed, he had breakfast ready. They saw the twins off to school together, then took care of the chores, had a quiet lunch, and on the days the girls didn't have kindergarten, they'd visit Harley and Gage. Afterwards, Jane would prepare supper while Mike enjoyed playtime with his daughters. Then everyone fell into bed exhausted.

Abby called Mike daily, grilling him like he was an axe murderer in disguise, and he always hung up the phone looking worried. It was obvious he loved his family so much. Why couldn't her sister leave him alone and let him get on with the rest of his life?

Jane's cell rang, dragging her out of her thoughts, and she saw it was her mom so she picked it up. "Hi Mom."

"How are you doing, honey?"

"Great. I'm making chili and cornbread for supper." She pulled open the oven door and set the cornbread in to bake. "How are you?"

"Your dad is going deaf. I want to buy one of those new TV's with the blue-fangs so he can use the headset, but he doesn't like change."

"You mean Bluetooth, Mom."

She snorted. "Bluetooth. Funny name. Maybe you could come set it up for us."

A scream of laughter came from the living room and Jane wondered what she was missing. "I have to go, Mom. Was there something you called about in particular?"

"No. I just wanted to hear your voice." Her mom's voice lowered to a whisper. "Are you sure everything is okay?"

"Better than okay." At another scream of laughter, she peered over her shoulder and realized that she was falling for this family. Her heart pinched and she turned her back on the noise and refocused on her mom. "I'll pop over for a visit after the storm passes, maybe tomorrow, and you can see for yourself."

"All right, honey. See you soon. I love you."

"I love you too, Mom." Jane thumbed the end button and disconnected the call, then tiptoed across the kitchen and peeked into the living room to see Laura and Lisa tussling on the floor. Mike glanced up and smiled that deep sexy grin he sometimes used on her when he was knee deep in his children's fun. Then the girls rolled over his legs, distracting him.

She smiled and retraced her steps across the kitchen, heading for the pantry in search of kidney beans to mix in with the chili. Pulling out a small stepladder hidden in the corner, she pulled it out and climbed onto the top rung to search through the cans on the higher shelves.

A noise at the doorway brought her around.

"Don't show Lisa the ladder," Mike said with a pained look and a shake of his head. "We'll find her in the top of a closet or on a bookshelf."

"Ah, that would explain why it's hidden behind the table extensions." As he stepped inside the tiny pantry, her heart did a pitter-patter and a thump. She turned back to the shelf because he was too close and her body was reacting in a rush of pure ecstasy.

His deep, sexy voice curled inside of her. "Is there something I can help you with?"

She shook her head, spotted a cake pan and mix on the top shelf, and reached for it. "No. You guys sounded like you were having so much fun and I just wanted to see what you were up to."

"You should join us."

"Someone needs to make supper." She spotted the cans of kidney beans and grabbing a couple, set them down with the cake pan and mix on a lower shelf so she could get down safely.

But as she turned around, Mike stepped forward and caught her hand. "Here, let me steady you so you don't fall."

It felt ridiculous to accept his help to get down two tiny steps, but the electrification of his hand touching hers made her want to be helpless and weak just so he'd continue to touch her. She stepped down one rung and stopped when they were on eye level.

They were standing close—too close—and his eyes searched her face. Then almost as though he couldn't help himself, he leaned in, holding her gaze with his. And then his lips met hers, soft at first, warm with desire and need.

And she couldn't help herself because she wanted so much more. Because it had been so long since she'd been touched like this, gentle and tender like she was more than a sexual thing.

She swayed toward him, deepening the kiss, loving the feel of his arms wrapped around her as he pulled her against his hard body.

The kiss was everything she remembered from the first night she'd spent in his house...and more. It was soft and gentle, and it made her want to climb up his big body and inhale all of him.

But when there was a giggle at the doorway, Mike smiled against her mouth and broke off the kiss. Wrapping one arm around her waist, he grabbed her other hand and lifted her off the bottom step. Pressed against the hard length of his body, it was all she could do to draw a breath.

He carefully set her down on her feet, and humming a tune, danced her out of the pantry, past the giggling girls, and into the living room. Jane couldn't help it...now she was laughing too and hanging on to him.

Someone turned on the radio, and within a few minutes, the girls had joined in and they were all having a dance party. Mike released her into Lisa's arms while he swept Laura off her feet and spun her around until they were both dizzy and laughing.

As the song came to an end, Mike released Laura and smoothly swept Jane back into his arms. She felt his whole body pressed against hers, big and strong and clingable, and when the last notes of the song finished, there was so much sizzle in his gaze that it scorched her from the inside out.

And scared her too. Only the buzz of the stove timer broke them apart. Jane stepped back, faked a no-nonsense attitude, and clapped her hands at the girls. "Okay everyone, go wash up for supper."

With one last look at her, Mike followed the girls to the bathroom where there was much splashing, more giggling, and the three of them came back into the kitchen looking a little soggy. She narrowed her eyes at them. "Did you wipe up the water?"

"Yes, Ma'am, we did," they replied in unison. Then they exchanged a surprised glance and the three of them burst out laughing.

They devoured the cornbread and chili, and ate fruit for dessert instead of the cake she had planned—and the thought of the cake warmed her cheeks and brought back memories of the kiss in the pantry and the dance while she'd been pressed flush against Mike.

By the time he had the girls bathed and ready for bed, she was done cleaning up the kitchen...and the urge to escape consumed her.

Mike was too precious. She would like nothing better than to climb onto the couch where he'd been sleeping and spend the night in his arms. But it was clear he was no more ready for a relationship than she was...was he?

And yet, as she came out from saying goodnight to the twins, as she crossed paths with him in the kitchen, he stopped her. He had one of those serious slants to his mouth that made her want to run for the hills...or kiss it away.

"I'm sorry," he said, and hooked a thumb toward the pantry. "I hope I wasn't out of line in there."

"No." She ducked her head and blushed, and when she

found the courage to peer back up at him, she stood up on her tiptoes, planted a quick kiss on his mouth, and said, "Good night."

Then she ran for the safety of her bedroom and closed the door.

A few minutes later, she heard something in the hallway. She opened the door just a crack and saw Mike standing in the doorway of the master bedroom like he was attempting to find the courage to step inside. Deciding he needed a private moment, and that she shouldn't be spying, she closed the door. As she did so, she saw him step inside.

And her heart sang out loud and clear. *I love you, Mike Toryn.*

She leaned back against the door and wondered if he'd now wait till she made the next move.

But could she do it without falling apart?

CHAPTER TWENTY-ONE

Mike woke in the comfort of his own bed, and for a moment he was somewhere between a dream world and the real world. He could hear Hannah's soft ladylike snores beside him. He could feel the warmth of her body within arm's reach.

But when he finally opened his eyes, he was alone…but surprisingly, not lonely.

He rolled onto his back, stared at the night-darkened ceiling, and whispered, "Forgive me, sweetheart." When there was no reply, he continued. "I didn't intend to, but I think I've fallen in love again. You were gone too early, too young. Please forgive me."

Still no answer, and now the guilt was stronger than ever.

He'd betrayed his wife. Betrayed her with a woman who in many ways seemed far more fragile than Hannah had ever been. Hannah, who had been fragile in health, but strong in spirit.

There was something about Jane that urged him to be careful, a skittishness that made him want to wrap her in his arms and protect her from the demons that haunted her memories. She hadn't had a nightmare since that first night she'd spent in his house, but her terrified scream had woken something in him that had died along with his wife.

And now he had to decide what to do about these feelings for her. If five or ten years had passed since Hannah's death, it would have been acceptable to fall in love again, but six months later...

He also had to consider Laura and Lisa. They were so young and he didn't want them to forget their mother. Yet they were far too young to be *without* a mother.

Mike forced himself out of bed to begin his day. It was still dark, so he fumbled around for his clothes with only the night light in the hall to guide him. He pulled on wool socks, jeans, a t-shirt, a long sleeved flannel shirt, and padded down the hallway past the bedrooms where everyone still slept. Then bundled up for the sub-zero weather, he headed out into the chilly morning through the freshly fallen snow toward the horse barn.

An hour later, he made his way back to the house to start breakfast. As his footsteps crunched across the new fallen snow, a light came on in the kitchen, blazing bright through the darkness, lighting his way toward his family. His heart sighed in his chest, and for the first time in what felt like forever, he realized that he was happy.

Laura always woke first—her internal alarm clock set to early, like his—and she woke up Lisa with a tickle and a song.

As he stepped into the house, quietly shutting the door behind him so as not to wake Jane, he could hear the pitter patter of tiny feet as the twins raced down the hallway and into the kitchen, Laura skipping to the table like a Disney princess while Lisa loped toward the porch in a near perfect imitation of her pony.

"*Daddy*," his youngest daughter screamed at the top of her voice, and no matter how many times he reminded her to use her inside voice, she was still over-the-top enthusiastic about everything…including, once again, him.

He tugged off his jacket and toed off his boots. "Hush, Munchkin. Jane is still sleeping."

"Oops, I forgot," she whispered as she grabbed his hand and tugged him toward the kitchen. "I helped Laura make her bed, then she helped me make mine." When he made a move to veer into the kitchen, she tugged him toward the table instead. "Did you see my homework? I colored *inside* the lines, Daddy. *Inside* like Jane told me to practice."

"Way to go, Munchkin," he said as he paused to take a good long look at her work.

She let go of his hand and climbed onto the chair, grabbed the red crayon, and promptly drew a squiggly line through the center of the page before giving him one of her full-toothed grins. "There. Signed by Lisa Toryn."

He grinned back at her. "Maybe you'll be a famous colorer one day."

Her eyes lit with excitement and turning to a new page, she got down to work coloring inside the lines.

Mostly.

Mike ruffled Laura's hair on the way by. "Good morning, Monkey."

She didn't raise her head, just grabbed him by the shirtsleeve knowing he would stop. "How many more, Daddy?"

Mike tried to be casual as he leaned over her to peer at the calendar on the table in front of her, as though it wasn't breaking his heart that she was counting the days till she could return to live with her uncle and aunt. "You count."

She turned an icy glare toward her sister. "I tried, but Lisa won't shut up, and then I lose count."

The guilty party raised her head. "Twelve, fifteen, twenty-two."

Laura sighed, clearly vexed. "See?"

"Okay, let's ignore your sister and do it together." He pointed to the first square without an X and started the count. "One. Two."

Laura joined in, while Lisa colored sometimes inside the lines and sometimes outside the lines and whispered random numbers in an attempt to muddle them up. And with each successive number, Mike wished he could turn back the calendar or slow down time, because it was all going by far too fast.

Earlier in the week, Harley's doctor had said that if everything looked good after the first trimester, the twins could return. Since hearing the news, Laura had started to count down the days, and he had a limited amount of time to win Abby and the twins over.

But he could do it. He *had to* do it. Otherwise he'd spend the rest of his days holed up on the ranch, alone and lonely.

When they finished the count, his oldest daughter tilted her head back so she could look at him, and a whisper of a smile played with the edges of her tiny mouth. "You're crooked upside down, Daddy."

He tweaked her nose and grinned. "I'm not crooked. You're the one who's crooked."

Lisa's voice rang out like a demented fire alarm. *"You're both crooked."*

Mike straightened, and when he saw her hanging upside down on her chair, he laughed softly. "Inside voice, Munchkin. Jane's still sleeping, remember?"

She happily zipped her mouth closed, tossed away the key, then sat up and resumed her *work*.

Laura tugged at his shirtsleeve, redrawing his attention, her dark eyes full of concern. "Forty-two days is a really long time, isn't it, Daddy? It's like almost to next summer."

"Not quite that long." He reached out with one finger to smooth the frown from between her perfectly formed eyebrows. "In my opinion, forty-two days isn't nearly long enough. I wish you didn't have to leave for another thirty-five *years* instead."

She peered up at him, solemn and considering and thoughtful, as though weighing his words, as though judging him. Mike tussled her hair and smiled. "Time for your old man to cook breakfast, Monkey. You don't want to be late for the school bus."

As she returned her attention to the calendar, and he headed into the kitchen, Jane staggered out of the hallway and moaned, "Coffee."

Mike grabbed the pot and stuck it under the tap. "It'll be ready in a jiff."

"Thank you." Tousled and sleepy-eyed, she slid onto the chair across from the twins, and around a yawn, greeted them. "Good morning, girls."

Lisa bounced up on the seat of her chair and held out the coloring book for Jane's inspection. "Look, Jane, I signed my name."

Mike turned off the tap and poured the water into the pot. In his peripheral vision, he could see Jane tilt her head as though intently studying the squiggles. Then she smiled, and the pure love and joy in that smile hit him square in the solar plexus.

"Beautifully done, darling," she said, unaware that as he spooned coffee grounds into the unit, he found himself falling deeper...deep and hard.

Across from her, Laura gathered up the calendar and slid it neatly under her chair. "Daddy wants us to live here for another thirty-five years."

"Only thirty-five?" She raised her gaze to him, and the softness in her eyes tilted his world off balance, and that's when he knew for sure. He could no more bear to let Jane go than he could bear to lose the girls again. "Well, I guess forty isn't too old to marry and have a family of your own, is it?"

Lisa rested her chin on her hand. "Forty is older than Daddy."

With a glint in her eyes, Jane leaned forward and said, "Not quite, but he'll probably need a cane on his next birthday anyway."

And as the girls giggled and Jane's smile deepened, Mike had to turn his back on them and tune out their conversation or he'd never get coffee made and breakfast on the table.

This was supposed to be his life with Hannah, he thought as he set the coffee pot to strong and pushed the ON button. His heart was bursting with love and breaking with sorrow, both as the same time. And now here was Jane, lifting his heart—lifting him—out of the ashes of his old life and into something new.

He pulled out eggs and bread and fruit, and as the girls chatted and the eggs sizzled and the toast popped, he filled juice glasses and coffee cups and wished this moment could last an eternity.

When he finally joined them at the table, Hannah's spot at the far end conspicuously empty, Laura glanced from the empty spot to him and awarded him with an unexpected smile that gave him a smidgen of hope that one day, she might stop counting the days on the calendar of her own free will.

After breakfast, there was a flurry of activity as the girls brushed their teeth. Mike and Jane gathered homework and backpacks and lunches. Then they all dressed for the chilly winter morning. As the four of them headed out to the road to wait for the bus, his heart filled with contentment and overflowed with love.

In a flurry of hugs and kisses and *have a great day*, the twins turned and ran toward the bus, calling out greetings to their friends and neighbors.

And as the bus doors closed behind them, taking his beautiful children away from him for the day, Mike whispered, "I love you both so very much."

Jane's hand slipped into his. "They love you too, you know."

He glanced over at her and casually stated, "Everything I love is at the end of this dirt road."

She didn't say *I love you* back. In fact, she didn't say anything. But there was a new softness in her gaze. And as the bus pulled away, they stood there and waved to the girls who were at one of the tiny windows waving back.

This is how he'd always imagined life. Filled with butterfly kisses, chubby arms, and the woman he loved to share it all with.

As the bus disappeared from sight, Jane pulled her hand free, turned to him, and flicked the rim of his cowboy hat. "So cowboy, what chores do you have lined up for us today?"

Everything that was right and good in his life was right there in her eyes.

As they turned back to walk down the lane together, the rising sun scuttled behind a cloud, and the promise of a bright day vanished the moment Jane's cell phone rang. With one look at the display screen, she stopped. The haunted look was back in her eyes.

She turned her back on him. "I need to take this. I'll catch up to you in a few."

And then she walked away, back up the snow-covered lane, out of earshot.

Mike let her go without a word, because maybe—just maybe—this is how it was all supposed to end.

CHAPTER TWENTY-TWO

By the end of the day, Jane was exhausted from the sheer effort of pretending that everything was okay, that nothing had changed since the phone call that morning, that her life wasn't about to take a nosedive into the public sphere.

Everything she ever wanted was right here on the Rocky Creek Ranch—home, love, family—and by tomorrow, it would all be gone.

Jane practiced smiling past the unshed tears, even though she knew her smile was too big and too fake, but she wanted them to remember her with laughter and joy, not sorrow and pity.

She poked her head into the bathroom.

Steam from the girls' hot bath covered the mirrors and hung in the air. In the tub, they were rosy cheeked and smiling. Bubbles and squirt toys bounced gently on the waves from their movements. "Almost done?"

Laura plopped a handful of suds on top of her sister's head. "Five more minutes, please?"

She wanted their last night together to be fun, so she nodded and grabbed a towel to wipe up the water on the floor. "Five more minutes and then it's time to get out. Your daddy will be back from the barn soon and then we'll sit down to watch a movie."

"Can we have popcorn?" Lisa asked as she stuck a blob of suds on her sister's chin, then giggled when it looked like a white beard.

"You bet." She hung up the towel and with tears stinging at the back of her eyes, she quickly left and headed to the kitchen where she grabbed the large frying pan, popcorn kernels, and oil.

There was a thump-thump-thump on the wood of the porch—Mike banging the snow off his feet—then the back door clicked open and clicked shut. A blast of icy air raced across her bare feet and made her shiver.

A couple of minutes later, he stepped into the kitchen, his cheeks ruddy from the cold, rubbing his hands together to warm them up.

"Sorry I dumped you with the dishes and twins." He raked a hand through his hair, looking tired. "I lost track of time."

"No problem. We're getting ready for movie night." She turned up the dimming wattage of her smile and poured a dollop of oil into the pan. He'd been in the north quarter earlier that afternoon and found an injured cow. "How's the patient?"

"Fine. I have her inside for the night. The vet will be here in the morning." There was silence, but she chose to ignore it and instead focused on getting a measuring cup from one of the higher shelves. When she couldn't reach it, he came around to help her. "Here, let me. I don't know why Hannah kept these things up so high."

As he came up behind her, resting one hand on her shoulder, leaning forward—into her, against her—to reach the tin cup, Jane closed her eyes and tried not to hyperventilate.

She knew exactly why his wife had put things up high. Because the lucky woman had known that her loving husband would see her struggle and be right there to help her, his long, lean body pressed against her, wakening every erogenous cell in her body.

She let her eyes drift shut so she could enjoy the sensation, and sent up a silent apology. *Sorry for lusting after your husband, Hannah, but it turns out, I'm human after all.*

When he stepped away and broke the physical contact, she blinked her eyes open and resumed breathing. Without looking at him for fear he would see everything in her eyes—lust, love, sadness—she took the cup and poured a healthy portion of kernels into it, then made the mistake of looking at him anyway.

His eyes flickered—just barely—and if she hadn't gotten to know him these last few weeks, she wouldn't have even noticed. But as she made to turn away, he captured her hand. "Jane, are you okay?"

She extracted her hand from his, careful to avoid any fast move for fear of giving away her agitation. "Of course. Just a little tired. Maybe I'm fighting off the flu."

His frown of contention turned up a notch. "You go climb into bed. I'll take care of the girls."

He had such kind, loving eyes. How could her sister not see how gentle and caring this man was?

"No, I'm okay." She set the cup aside and turned to retrieve butter out of the fridge, but Mike was standing in her way. "Excuse me, please."

He gave her a funny look. "We promised not to lie to each other, Jane."

Damn. She should have had her fingers crossed behind her back that day. Pressing her lips together, she tried to step around him, but he blocked her way—big, dangerous to her heart, so gentle and kind. She was about to stomp on his heart and she hated herself for it.

But she didn't have a choice. She gritted her teeth. "Mike, you're in my way."

Mouth thin, he shifted to allow her to step around him, and when she had her head deep in the fridge, when the tears would no longer hold off and she had to blink rapidly so they wouldn't spill down her cheeks and give her away, she pretended that she couldn't find the butter, rearranging things, fussing, her butt sticking out like some teen who had only been away from the table for ten seconds.

His voice came from behind, deep and quiet. "Who called you this morning? What did they want?"

Jane grabbed the butter, straightened, slammed the door shut, then instantly regretted her show of anger. "Nobody, Mike. It was nothing."

Keeping her head lowered so he wouldn't see the sheen in her eyes, she pretended to be focused on unwrapping the butter as she brushed past him.

She didn't want their last night together to be like this, angry and hurtful and evasive. She wanted it to be peaceful and fun, maybe some cuddling after the twins were in bed…maybe something more.

But they were both getting hot under the collar. She could feel the atmosphere in the kitchen change from warm and cozy to heated and angry.

Then his voice turned soft and gentle. "Don't you think I know you by now? Your moods, the light in your eyes, the phoniness in your smile."

She attempted to ignore him. Poured oil into the pan.

Kernels into the oil.

His voice lowered more. "Look at me, Jane." And when she made the mistake of doing just that, he said, "I love you. Please trust me enough to let me help you."

There was a scream from the bathroom and they both jumped. She started past him. "I should go—"

Mike caught her by the upper arm and she froze. He rubbed the other hand across the back of his neck, his gaze on her intense as though he could see into her soul, before he let his gaze dip to the popcorn. "I'll let you finish here while I get the girls out of the tub."

Jane couldn't stand the pain and confusion in his eyes. Turning so she faced him directly, she placed one palm against the middle of his chest, felt the warmth of his body seep into her ice cold hand, the steady thud of his heart making her wish she could curl into his arms, lay her head on his chest, and listen to the comforting beat until it was time to leave.

When she opened her mouth, she wasn't even sure what would come out. "I'm sorry, Mike. I want us to have a nice night together. I don't want to argue with you."

He covered her hand with his and opened his mouth to say something, but there was another scream. Instead, he smiled, crooked. "I'll leave you to the popcorn making then, and get the girls before they flood the house."

But she knew by the intensity of his gaze that the reprieve from his inquisition was only temporary.

She watched him leave, and when she heard the bathroom door close with him inside, the tears came. She had to grab a tissue, blow her nose, and give herself a lecture. Then she washed her hands, turned to the stove, and turned on the burner.

By the time the popcorn was in a bowl and buttered, the

girls were out of the bathroom, dressed and bounding into the kitchen like a couple of frisky colts. Mike followed at a slower pace, and by the look on his face, she knew that he was still focused on the falseness in her smile

"Jane, we bathed ourselves," Laura announced proudly.

"Good girls." She smiled and held up the bowl. "Popcorn's ready. Movie is set up to go."

Lisa screamed, "*Beauty and the Beast.*"

And when the twins raced off, Jane and Mike followed silently.

They sat on the couch, Mike's arm on the back, the twins seated between them with the popcorn bowl on their laps, all tucked in and cozy under a warm blanket. She reached out to brush something off the back of Lisa's hair, and Mike caught her hand in his, laced their fingers together, his eyes soft and worried. And even though Jane forced herself to look away, back to the big screen TV, she couldn't bring herself to break off the physical contact.

It was peaceful and beautiful and she wished it could go on forever.

By the end of the movie, a few tears had escaped, but she blamed it on the happily-ever-after ending. The girls bought her story. Mike didn't.

She dashed away the tears and forced herself to be efficient. "Your daddy is going to tuck you in, so I'll just say goodnight now."

Hugging them, wishing she didn't have to let them go—ever—she pushed to her feet and said, "They're all yours. I'm turning in now. Goodnight."

She was aware of his gaze on her until she disappeared behind the closed bedroom door. She showered and walked past the bedroom once, saw Mike squished between the two girls, reading them their nighttime story, one arm around each girl as they cuddled against his big body, making Jane extremely jealous of the fact that she couldn't do the same.

She climbed into bed, pulling the covers up to her chin to ward off the chill of the evening, ears straining for the sounds of the people she'd started to think of as her family—hearing the twins say goodnight, listening to Mike's soft tread as he left their bedroom and went into his own—until finally, the house descended into total silence.

A tear spilled and she dashed it away, then acknowledged that she wouldn't sleep tonight.

No, what she wanted to do was spend her last night here in Mike's arms, a memory to hold onto after the awful truth came out and he could no longer stand to look at her. So she climbed out of bed, opened the bedroom door with barely a squeak of the hinges, and crossed the hallway.

There was a soft glow coming from his bedroom, so she knew he was still awake. She paused in the doorway and he glanced up from the book he was reading. He was sitting on the bed, his lower body covered by the blankets, his upper body naked and golden in the glow of the bedside lamp.

She entered the room, closed the door, and ventured closer, taking in the width of his broad shoulders, the way his skin looked so smooth over the hardness of muscles strengthened by hours laboring on the ranch. He set the book aside on the table, his gaze steady on her face, and when she reached the side of the bed, he captured her hand and lifted it to his lips and kissed the inside of her palm.

His lips were warm, his hands warm too, and she sat down on the edge of the bed, hip to hip with him.

His voice was low and rough, like he hadn't used it in forever. "Are you sure?"

That was all the confirmation she needed. She leaned into him, pressed her mouth against his. He tasted of the coffee he'd drank after supper. He tasted like forever.

And then he was sliding down on the bed, and she was climbing in beside him, absorbing the heat of his body, the gentleness of his touch, as though right at that very moment, she was the most precious thing in the world.

He lifted his mouth from hers and said, "I love you."

Then there was no more time for words, only action. The slide of his hand across her breast, over her hip. The smoothness of his skin under her hands. The strength of his body over hers.

When he slid into her, it was all she could do to draw a breath, then after, when she finally had her ear pressed to his chest, she memorized his slow deep breaths as he fell asleep, the steady thump of his heart, the way they fit together so perfectly.

"I love you," she whispered back.

In the wee hours of the morning, long before he woke up, she extracted herself from his arms and returned to her room where she quickly packed her few belongings, then went to kiss the girls goodbye. Stopping in the doorway of the master bedroom, she drank in the sight of him, the glow of the moon cutting him in sharp angular strength. And then she forced herself to leave before she changed her mind.

Not that she could. She had to testify in court, and by tomorrow this time, there would be no question about coming back because Mike wouldn't want her anywhere near him or his daughters.

In the kitchen, she turned on the flashlight app on her iPhone, dug a notepad out of a drawer, located a pen among Lisa's crayons, and sat down at the table to write him a note.

A simple note, before she caved into the desire to stay.

Dear Mike...I cannot properly express my gratitude for the time I've spent with you and Laura and Lisa. You saved my life and my mind, and I will forever treasure my time here.

I know you'll work things out with Abby. You're a good daddy...

She wrote quickly, from the heart, and managed to stay dry eyed until she was out in the cold night air with Pepper saddled. As she mounted and headed back to her parents' ranch to return to the nightmarish reality of her life, the tears finally overflowed.

God, she was going to miss them all so very much. But she had no choice. She had to leave before the truth came out...before they could reject her.

There was only one thing left to do. Get on that stand, hold her head up high, tell the truth, and hope for justice.

Afterwards, she'd put Mike and the girls and the past behind her, and trust that all would be right in the end...even if she was alone.

CHAPTER TWENTY-THREE

Mike slept like a man with no more demons and no more regrets.

It was the first solid sleep he'd had since Hannah had received her prognosis, and for the first time in months, he woke feeling well rested, happy, and eager for the new day to start.

He rolled onto his back, glanced over to the other side of the bed expecting to see Jane there, but she was already gone, probably back to her own bed to protect the girls.

Cupping his hands behind his head, he remained right where he was, the memory of making love with her seared into his brain like braille on a blind man's book.

She'd brought him out of the darkness and back into the light. For the first time in what seemed like forever, he could see the future in a positive light. Jane at his side. Maybe another addition or two to their family. The twins growing up, attending university, marrying and having a family of their own one day.

He knew without question that Jane would *love* being a grandma.

The subtle scent of her was on his skin, on his pillow, on the sheets, surrounding him in the warmth of her love. Even though she hadn't said the words yet, he was positive that her feelings for him were as strong as his were for her.

Down the hallway, a door creaked open, and as he heard the pitter patter of tiny feet racing his way, he glanced at the alarm clock.

He'd slept in an entire hour past the twins' normal get up time.

Yesterday he would have panicked at the thought of the girls missing the bus, knowing full well that he'd have Abby on his case. But today, he didn't care. Today was a day for celebration and joy, and if they had to rush a wee bit, or if he had to drive the twins into town for kindergarten, then listen to a lecture from Abby about parental responsibility…well, today he had the patience for a thousand lectures from the social worker.

The twins raced into his bedroom, scrambled onto the bed, and while Lisa started to jump up and down on the mattress, adorably dressed in her pink ballerina outfit from last Halloween, Laura, still in her pajamas, scrambled across the king size bed.

"Daddy, *get up.*"

Mike grinned at his too serious daughter. "Good morning, Sunshine."

She straddled his body and went nose to nose with him. "You don't understand. We're going to be late for school."

With another smile, he tickled her on the ribs and was rewarded with a giggle before he rolled her off him, then threw back the covers and sat up, thankful he'd pulled his boxers on before he'd drifted off to sleep last night, equally thankful for the jeans he'd left within arm's reach. He kept his voice quiet. "We're going to let Jane sleep in this morning, so be extra quiet while you go back to your room and get dressed."

As he bent to pull on his socks, Lisa tackled her sister and their heads knocked together.

Laura rubbed her forehead and glared at her sister. "But Daddy, Jane will be sad if we don't say goodbye."

It was true, she would be. He knew in his gut that Jane loved the girls as much as he did. Reluctantly, he agreed. "But we have to be tiptoe quiet, okay?"

The girls nodded, and after he quickly dressed, they followed him down the hallway to her bedroom where he knocked on the door.

Silence came from the other side.

Laura tugged at his belt loop and whispered, "Open the door, Daddy."

For the first time since waking, he felt a sense of trepidation and a tightness in his chest. He swung open the door, saw her bed neatly made, and the pile of clothes she kept on the chair gone. "Maybe she's in the kitchen making breakfast."

But even as the words spilled out of his mouth, he knew it wasn't true. With the school clock ticking down, he pulled the door shut and urged the girls toward the kitchen.

Laura's feet didn't move. "Where's Jane?"

Heart in his throat, he gazed down at the ornery girl.

Ever since the head collision, her mood had been going sideways, and now it seemed to have gotten worse. He put one hand on Laura's back, and one on Lisa's, and gave them each a gentle nudge down the hallway. "She probably went to see her mom. She's been so busy helping us out that she hasn't had time to see her parents."

Lisa gazed up at him with a frown. "Then why are her clothes gone?"

His children were, if nothing else, persistent and observant. "Good question. While you're at school, I'll figure it out."

Laura glared back at him. "I want to help find Jane."

"They're expecting you at school, honey."

All the way to the kitchen table, Lisa pushed at Laura, and Laura shoved back. And when he finally got them seated at the table—Lisa once again coloring outside the lines, Laura counting the days on her calendar—he went into the kitchen to make something quick for breakfast.

As he headed toward the fridge, he checked his phone for a message.

Nothing.

Behind him, Lisa's voice rang out. "I'm helping you make breakfast, Daddy."

Mike turned to find his youngest daughter standing on the countertop, her pink tutu gently bouncing up and down as she hopped from foot to foot. She had the cupboard door open and was pulling out plates and glasses. He swooped her up into his arms, carried her back to the table, and plunked her down on a chair. "Stay put."

Her golden gaze shone with innocence. "But I'm hungry."

Outside, there was a roar of the school bus and a honk of the horn as it stopped in front of their driveway.

Laura jumped to her feet and ran to the window, her voice a grumble. "We're missing the bus. We never miss the bus when Jane is here."

Mike took in his daughters—Laura still in her pjs, Lisa now attempting a pirouette on the seat of her chair—and glanced at the clock. "There's still lots of time to drive you to school."

Down the lane, the school bus roared away.

Given their limited time, he faced the girls, hands on hips, tone firm. "Go get washed and dressed while I make breakfast."

They ran off, pushing and shoving at each other, and Mike turned his attention to the stove. And that's when he noticed the note beside the coffee machine. Lisa must have pushed it aside while she was pulling down plates.

He picked it up. It was Jane's handwriting. Clean, crisp, efficient.

Dear Mike...I cannot properly express my gratitude for the time I've spent with you and Laura and Lisa. You saved my life and my mind, and I will forever treasure the time I've spent with your precious family.

I know you'll work things out with Abby. You're a good daddy, and anyone who sees you with the twins can discern that immediately. So maybe invite my sister to come stay with you for a few days so she can see firsthand. God knows, she could use some time away from her job to decompress and destress.

And who knows. Maybe the two of you will fall in love, get married, and grow your family. Beneath that tough exterior, Abby is a kind and gentle woman who means well and is only putting the needs of the children above all else...as she should.

Please give the girls my love. I'll miss them as much as I'll miss you.

Above all else, thank you for allowing me to join your family and be normal for a short time.

All my love,

Jane.

Mike glared at the words on the paper, wishing them away, but as the letters began to squiggle and distort, and the moisture in his eyes threatened to spill over, there was an uproar coming from the twins' bedroom.

He crumpled the note in his hand, stuffed it into the front pocket of his jeans, and headed out of the kitchen.

By the time he got to the bedroom, Lisa's nose was bleeding and Laura wore her pissed off expression. She yelled, "She wouldn't be like this if Jane was here."

All the doubts he had as a single dad returned.

What if Laura was right? What if it had been Jane's presence that had brought harmony back into his family? What if he couldn't make a happy home for his daughters without her?

Had last night been Jane's way of saying goodbye because she didn't want to be part of this family?

His heart cracked, but if he'd learned one thing since Hannah's death, it was that the twins had to come first…and that he had to raise them with or without anyone else's help.

His phone rang. Praying it was Jane, he tugged it out of his shirt pocket and thumbed the ON button. To the twins, he said, "Shush."

Only then did he see Abby's name on the screen. Before he could say a word, she demanded, "What did you do to my sister?"

His heart picked up its pace. "You know where Jane is?"

There was a scream behind him—Laura pulling Lisa's hair—and he chose to ignore it for the moment.

But not Abby. "What's going on there?"

"Nothing," he said as one handed, he tried to separate the twins. He stepped between them, grabbed Lisa around the waist to prevent her from going after her sister, and repeated his question. "Have you seen Jane?"

And then he felt this hand numbing pain in his wrist. He

dropped the phone, and dislodged Lisa's teeth from his wrist. "Why are you biting me?"

Her growl sounded like something from a horror movie. "I'm a zombie." Then she smiled up at him and spoke in her clear, sweet voice. "I'm hungry, Daddy. Let's go make breakfast."

"In a sec, sweetheart." He could hear Abby's voice near his feet. Reaching down, he grabbed the phone, straightened, carried Lisa with him to the kitchen so she couldn't turn around and go after her sister. "Abby? I'll call you back when I get the twins to school."

"They missed the bus?" There was something ominous in her tone.

"It's no big deal," he said as he glanced at the time and realized that they were going to be late for school too.

"I want you, the girls, and Gage in my office at ten today."

The bad feeling in his gut worsened. "The girls have school—"

Lisa started wiggling in his arms and when he wouldn't release her, she opened her mouth and screamed bloody murder.

On the other end of the call, Abby raised her voice. "Oh, for crying out loud, they're in kindergarten. They can miss a day of school. Be here or be sorry."

And then she disconnected the call.

As Mike tucked the cell back into his shirt pocket, Laura slipped in front of him, pulled back her arm, and punched him in the stomach. He doubled over in surprise. "What the hell?"

Eye level, she got into his face and shouted, "It's your fault Jane is gone."

And while Mike struggled to maintain some semblance

of order, he tried to dress the girls, tried to brush and braid their hair, tried to feed them breakfast—which incidentally, no one, including him, ate—but without Jane, nothing *felt* right.

In the end, Lisa refused to take off her ballerina costume, Laura's braid resembled a knot, and he couldn't help but wonder if Abby was right.

By ten o'clock, they were seated in Abby's office, all of them miserable and cranky and out of sorts. Gage had left work to join them, and it was clear right from the moment he walked in that the social worker was pissed.

Well, so was he.

Jane was gone, leaving behind nothing more than a *thank you* note and three broken hearts.

Since getting off the phone with Abby, he'd been trying to reach Jane, but she wasn't picking up his calls, or returning his each-one-more-desperate-than-the-last voice messages. And because he couldn't get through to her, the twins grew more pissy and upset.

Laura continued to accuse him of chasing Jane away, and Lisa's badness multiplied by leaps and bounds. And he swore, never again would he bring a woman into their lives. First Hannah, then Jane. And they'd both left him.

It was too hard, far too devastating to be worth the pain and disappointment. In that regard, it was far better to be alone.

Right this very moment in the social worker's office, Laura was sitting on the chair between Gage and him. Back stiff, body even stiffer, she answered all of Abby's questions in monotone syllables.

"Honey, are you happy being back with your daddy?"

"No."

"Do you want me to put you elsewhere?"

"Yes."

Meanwhile, Lisa wiggled and squiggled on his lap in her cute little ballerina outfit until she finally slipped free to tear around the room, making loud noises like a hotrod car on the racetrack. Mike pushed to his feet to catch her, his focus split between his youngest daughter, his oldest daughter, and the determined woman seated on the other side of the desk. "Abby, you can't take them away from me."

Abby glared at him like he was lower than pond scum. "If I think they're being mistreated or uncared for, I most certainly can."

He lunged for Lisa, but she was like a slippery newborn foal. "You know Harley is on bed rest, don't you?"

"Of course. There *are* other options."

And right at that very moment, for the second time in his life, everything went south. "What do you mean by other options?"

As Lisa raced past again, he lunged for her, and this time he caught her. She bucked and whacked her head on the corner of the bookshelf.

As she started howling, Laura started crying too. "Don't hurt my sister. I hate you."

In that moment, as both girls cried and chaos prevailed, Mike wanted to cry too.

Abby pushed to her feet, her eyes hard, her face void of expression, and above the noise said, "Gage, take the girls out of here so I can discuss this situation privately with Mike. I'll find someone to take care of them—maybe my parents—until I get this sorted out."

For just a moment, as Gage took hold of Laura's hand and swept Lisa into his arms, Mike exchanged a look with his brother, a look that offered support but was filled with pity and dread.

"Keep your cool, bro."

As soon as the door shut behind them, and the girls' cries grew quieter as they moved down the hallway, Mike turned to Abby to defend himself, wishing briefly he could drown his sorrows in a bottle of whiskey, then realizing that wasn't the path he was intended to take.

He turned to the social worker to attempt to reason with her. "It's not usually like that. They're upset because Jane left."

Thin lipped, Abby grabbed a big rubber stamp, snapped open an ink pad, and ground the stamp into the pad. "They're better off in a foster home."

Then she stamped the file.

Mike froze. "You can't do that."

She slapped the file shut. "Watch me."

Mike fisted his hands at his sides, remembering Gage's words. "What's your problem with me?"

Her silence reigned heavy in the room and he wondered if she would answer him, or just have the security people physically remove him.

Finally, she looked at him. "What did you do to my sister?"

His cheeks instantly heated.

No way was he telling her that he'd made love with Jane. Besides, Jane had left him, not the other way around. He *wouldn't* leave her, not ever. "Nothing. Why?"

Abby placed her hands palm down on the desktop. "She's been crying since she returned to the ranch."

Hope sprang to life inside of Mike.

He'd been calling her cell every five minutes, but she wasn't picking up. "She's at your parents' place?"

"Not any longer. She left for court this morning."

Now he was confused. "Court?"

Abby pushed to her feet. She still wore that pissed expression that boded ill for his situation, but now she appeared more cautious, like she'd said something she hadn't intended. "She didn't tell you?"

And now he was pissed. Jane had been lying by omission all along? "What court case?"

Abby sat down at the desk, grabbed another file, and refused to look at him. "We're done here."

"No, we're not." Mike placed his hands on the desk and got into her face. "Tell me what's going on."

She raised her gaze, her face void of emotion. "Why?"

Why indeed? He resolved to put everything on the line, including his heart. "Because I love your sister and I think she loves me too. Because I love my children and they love Jane. Because somehow, we've become a damn family, Abby, and you can't keep us apart."

He was desperate, sounded desperate, but at this particular moment, he didn't care.

She studied him for a moment, like a scientist might study a bug under a microscope, then with a shrug, returned her attention to the file on her desk. "If you want to know, Google it. The prosecuting lawyers tried to keep it quiet, but someone leaked it to the press this morning."

Mike straightened, his cell already in his hands. About to walk out the door, he faced her, and softened his voice and his attitude. "You are *not* taking my daughters away from me this time, Abby. I'm not the same man I was last spring. I understand now how precious my girls are. What a gift Hannah left in my care. I won't screw up this second chance to be their dad."

He turned on his heel and walked out, focused on the screen of his cell. And when he saw a picture of Jane walking up the steps of the courthouse, he stopped right in the middle of the hallway to skim the article...and he suddenly understood everything he needed to know about the woman he'd fallen in love with.

Someone bumped into him from behind and Abby growled, "Get out of my way, you big lug."

On leaden feet, Mike started down the hallway, his focus still on the news story. As she tried to squeeze past him, he stumbled to a stop and turned to confront her. "Jane didn't tell me."

"Of course she didn't tell you," the social worker snapped as she wiggled between him and the wall, and headed for the foyer. "She's ashamed. She believes that if people know what happened, they'll shun her. She refuses professional help. She won't even talk to me."

Hearing the crack in her voice, Mike followed on her heels, anger slowly working through the dazed part of his brain. "Why aren't you with her today? She needs your support."

As they entered the reception area, Mike saw his brother attempting to deal with the twins. Lisa sat on his shoulders, tugging on the lobes of his ears as though playing some musical instrument while she sang at the top of her lungs. Meanwhile, Laura stood in front of Gage, arms crossed over her chest, the familiar scowl on her face as she glared up at him.

His brother appeared totally out of his league, harried to the point of abandoning everything and everyone. And Mike realized that even though Gage and Harley had made the transition to parenting look easy, it wasn't any easier for them than it was for anyone else...including him.

Abby grabbed Lisa off his brother's shoulders and shouted, "*Quiet.*"

And the room went pin-drop quiet.

Lisa with her eyes wide and wild, and her mouth in a silent *oh*.

Laura with trepidation tensing her body as she eyed the suddenly scary social worker.

Mike knelt beside his oldest daughter and put one arm around her shoulders, casual and familiar and not giving a damn about whether Abby liked it or not. "What's up, Monkey?"

The older-by-two-minutes twin turned to face him. "Uncle Gage refuses to tell us what's going on, so I'm staring at him and Lisa is singing her annoying song, and we'll keep doing it until he cracks and tells all."

"I'll tell you," he said. He stood up, pulled Lisa out of Abby's arms, and stood her up beside her sister. Then he knelt down on one knee in front of them, only glancing up to ensure that the social worker was paying full attention. She was, so he refocused on the twins. "Since Aunt Harley is still recovering, you girls can't go with Uncle Gage. Instead, you're going with Abby. She'll probably take you back home and make you pack your things so she can take you away from me again—"

The social worker muttered, "Good plan."

Mike ignored her. "—but this time, I'm not going to let that happen. From here on out, we're in this together."

With a frown, Laura crossed her arms, suspicious as a teenage girl being conned into her mother's dress shop. "In *what* together?"

He shrugged and remained calm despite the racing of his heart and the urge to grab his girls and make a run for it. Straight for Jane. Bypass all the heartache and confusion. "Life. Loving each other and taking care of each other. Growing up and making sure that we never forget your mommy."

Lisa slid onto his knee and looped her arms around his neck. "Where are you going, Daddy?"

His heart thumped at her trusting nature. Too soon, she'd be grown up and ready to tackle life on her own, and she wouldn't need him like she needed him now. "To see Jane."

There was a definite easing in Laura's tiny body. "Can we come?"

"Not this time. This time I need to talk to her alone."

Lisa slid off his knee and crossed the foyer to stand beside Abby. She slipped her hand into the social worker's hand, her expression open and honest and serious as she addressed the woman who held their future in the palm of her hand. "My daddy loves my mommy, but his heart is big enough for Jane and Laura and me too. You'll see."

And even though there was doubt on his oldest daughter's face, when she crossed the foyer to join her sister, there was hope in her eyes too.

CHAPTER TWENTY-FOUR

They called it survivor's guilt and today, as Jane sat in the courtroom ready to testify against the monster who had captured, raped, and murdered the six women she'd befriended without ever seeing them face-to-face, the guilt of her own survival crushed against her chest.

The ordeal had been life changing, and in the months since she'd been rescued, she'd been closed mouthed, refusing to talk to anyone about the things she'd done to stay alive. Awful things, with a man she'd hated at first, then later bonded with because he'd kept her alive. Even now, seated in the courtroom with her captor in plain view, she felt a softening toward him that turned her stomach and made her hate herself.

For a moment, she wished she hadn't asked her parents and sister to stay away. She could have used their support. People who loved her despite her mistakes and her flaws and all of the horrible things she'd done throughout her days of trying to stay alive. *They* would never allow her to get up and walk out of the courtroom. *They* would make sure she was strong enough to testify and put the guilty party behind bars.

Almost as though he could sense her gaze, he turned his head and looked directly at her. She could feel herself fall into that downward spiral that always made her do whatever he demanded. And when he smiled at her and blew her a kiss, her heart skipped a beat and her breath snagged in her throat.

Jane dropped her gaze to her lap and clenched her hands into fists. She could feel her nails bite into her palms, and she relished the pain because it meant she was alive.

Alive and free.

She'd read about other victims who'd given in to this strange bond between captive and captor and refused to testify...

"The prosecution calls Jane Watts to the stand."

Frozen and terrified, tears pooled in her eyes and panic clutched tight around her lungs.

She wouldn't.

She couldn't.

"The prosecution calls Jane Watts to the stand."

A hand squeezed her shoulder, reassuring and supportive, and she pushed to her feet and walked to the witness stand without looking at anyone. As she raised her hand to be sworn in, the person who had been seated behind her snagged her attention. For a split second, she looked right into the eyes of the man she loved—Mike, the man who'd shared his family and his life with her for a few precious weeks—before she regrouped and refocused on the court clerk.

Because having the accused put away for his crimes was far more important than her instinct to protect herself. It was far more important than her need for love or family or the future.

She raised her hand, listened to the court clerk swear her in, and said, "I do."

Then Jane sat down, folded her hands on her lap, took a deep breath, and composed herself, ready to tell the awful truth to this courtroom of strangers…all strangers but one whom she loved with all her heart.

The man who could never love her back, not once he heard the truth of her ordeal.

The prosecuting lawyer stepped forward and stopped in front of the jury's bench. "Miss Watts, thank you for coming today—"

She knew the drill and she focused on the lawyer, on the compassion in his gaze, the determination too. Ever since he'd approached her, ever since he'd learned the truth about her ordeal and convinced her to testify, he'd been her champion.

Hands clasped on her lap, she took a deep breath, exhaled, then found herself staring instead into the eyes of the man she loved. And she couldn't look away. Once he knew the truth, she'd see the revulsion in his eyes, and then she could walk away and start out fresh, someplace where no one knew her name or her face.

"—please tell the court about your captivity."

She leaned forward, toward the microphone, inhaled…and the words tumbled out because she couldn't hold them back anymore. "My parents always said never to take rides from strangers, but on that day, I didn't listen."

"Is the man who gave you a ride that day in the courtroom?"

She shifted her gaze toward the man in the wrist and ankle cuffs, and recognized the twisted, sick murderer he was. "Yes."

"Please point him out."

For just a fraction of a second, she was back inside the damp darkness of the cold metal container. At his mercy. Willing to do anything he said so she could survive.

Then she blinked out of the moment, raised her arm, and pointed directly at him. "That's him."

The lawyer stepped between her and the murderer, and she blinked and focused on the prosecuting attorney and slowly lowered her arm.

"Miss Watts, I'd like you to tell the jury exactly what he did to you and the other women he kept prisoner."

Jane forced herself to face the women and men in the jury box, forced herself not to cringe away from their scrutiny and judgment. "I got lost. I still don't know exactly where I was, but one of my rear tires blew and my cell phone was dead. Then *he* came along and offered assistance. A ride to his farm just over the hill and around the corner. The use of his phone. He even had fresh coffee in his truck."

She closed her eyes, envisioning the terror of the next few hours, the next few days, the weeks that stretched into months. She forced her eyes open. Forced herself to get the rest of the story out before her courage faded and her throat went dry. "By the time I came to, I was naked and chained up in a container…"

CHAPTER TWENTY-FIVE

It seemed like hours later that the judge called for a recess. By the time Jane finished her testimony and the prosecutor turned her over to the defense lawyer for questioning, she was done feeling guilty for surviving when the other women had not been so lucky. All she wanted to do now was go home and move on with her life. Past the pain and the memories that had followed her everywhere for the past few months.

The court staff had been kind enough to offer her a private room where she could take a break without being bothered. So when she heard a knock on the door, she assumed it was one of the staff sent to bring her back to the courtroom.

Instead, when the door opened, Mike walked in. His gaze never left her face as he shut the door behind himself. "Why didn't you tell me, Jane?"

Hands clenched together, she gave a hoarse laugh. "I was afraid if I opened my mouth, everything would tumble out. The truth, the ugliness, the awful things I had to do to stay alive."

A frown twitched at his brow. "I can handle the truth, honey. What I can't handle is the thought of you walking away because you think you're not worthy of my love or anyone else's."

Love. She'd never realized how much she needed to be loved until she met this man. But she couldn't take him down with her. "You were a nice distraction, Mike. You and the girls. But it's better if we end things now, before they get truly ugly."

He closed the distance between them, the expression on his face full of something she couldn't quite identify. As he neared, she took an involuntary step back, fear momentarily overtaking the certainty that this man would never hurt her. And he stopped, immediately stepped back, giving her room—all the space she needed to realize that she didn't want space between them, not ever again.

"I love you, Jane Watts. I don't care what you had to do to survive. Nobody who loves you cares about what you did." His voice softened. "You're alive. You're here. We're together. That's all that matters now."

Her bottom lip trembled and she had to fight to control the tears. "It's going to be in all of the papers, Mike. Everyone will know the truth, and when the trial is over, I'll have to leave."

He gritted his teeth, fisted his hands at his sides. "You did nothing wrong, Jane."

And with her gaze fixed solemnly on his face, determination in her voice, she said, "It's over, Mike. I know it's not easy to accept. It's not easy for me either, but I'm doing what I believe is best for you and the girls." No longer able to look at the hurt in his beautiful eyes, she turned her back on him. "This is how it has to be. Now, if you could show yourself out, I'd like a few minutes alone before I have to go back on the stand."

She closed her eyes against the overwhelming silence in the room, praying that he would leave, praying equally hard that he would stay. Then she heard the soft tread of his boots against the tiled floor as he departed.

From the doorway, his quiet voice reached out to her. "After Hannah died, I never thought I'd love anyone again. But then you rode into my life and took root in my heart." He paused, but she refused to turn around. "Love doesn't come around often. Don't lose this chance because you're afraid."

And then he walked out.

Jane turned as soon as she heard the door click closed.

A moment later, one of the staff opened the door. "We're ready to resume."

When Jane walked into the courtroom, she couldn't help but search for Mike, but he was gone.

And she was left with a big hole in her chest where her tender heart had once been.

CHAPTER TWENTY-SIX

Mike returned to the ranch, aware that the trial would be over soon, aware that if he didn't do something fast, Jane would vanish and he'd never see her again.

As he stepped into the house and followed the quiet voices to the bedroom, he found Abby with the girls packing their things.

She raised her head, met his gaze, and her eyes were hard as ice chips. "Do I have to get a restraining order?"

"No." He crossed the room, sat down on one of the child-sized chairs at the small table, and fiddled with the plastic tea set, uncertain where to start. All he knew was that he had to talk to the girls, but he hoped Abby would hear too. "I saw Jane today. She's very sad she left us, and she doesn't believe we want her."

The twins immediately stopped packing and Abby stopped a heartbeat later.

A tiny frown formed between Laura's brows. "Why not?"

"She had some very bad things happen to her, things that make her feel unworthy of our love." He paused and took a deep breath. "That's how I felt when I couldn't save your mommy. Like I'd failed her and failed you girls. Like I didn't deserve your love. Like I didn't deserve to be happy ever again."

The girls moved closer. Lisa climbed onto his lap. Laura stopped in front of him, her hand on his knee. Tears filled his eyes. "Your mommy left you for me to take care of and I failed, but I'm not failing this time. I love you both so much and if you give me a second chance, I'll do better. I promise."

Laura tucked her small hand into his and Lisa laid her head into the crook of his neck. His voice grew hoarse. "Jane needs us too. She needs us to be a family again, and she needs to be part of our family."

Laura glanced toward Abby and everything in Mike stopped as he raised his gaze to Jane's sister. His words were soft and heartfelt. "Please don't break us apart. We need each other as much as Jane needs us."

Abby looked from him to each girl, then sighed. "Oh, what the hell." She moved forward and crouched down in front of the girls. "Is this what you want? To live with your daddy, even if Jane *doesn't* come live with you?"

In unison, Laura and Lisa said, "Yes."

And when Abby nodded her head, giving her consent, Laura threw herself into Mike's open arms, whispering into his ear, "Daddy, I love you."

His heart swelled with joy and his throat closed while he hugged her back. "I love you too, Monkey."

Abby stood up, made the universal *I'm watching you* sign, then left him alone with his family.

Mike knew that no matter what happened in the future, nothing—absolutely nothing—would ever cause him to mess up his family again.

He pulled back so he could gaze at their precious faces. "We're a package, a team, and no matter what, I will always be here for you."

Laura loosened her arms from around his neck and looked him in the eye. "Can we go get Jane now?"

"You bet."

He just hoped she loved them as much as they loved her.

CHAPTER TWENTY-SEVEN

Jane sat in the courtroom and waited for the jury to return with their verdict.

Now that it was all in the open, she didn't feel so much heaviness in her chest. For the first time in months, she felt like she could breathe.

Her cell had been vibrating steady—news reporters, magazine editors, even a movie director—but she wasn't interested in any of that. She just wanted to live a quiet life with family who accepted her and her past.

The only person she wanted to hear from now was Mike, but he hadn't called, not once since she'd told him to go away.

Her reasoning had been sound. The twins didn't need to be subjected to her past. And yet, now that she had spoken the truth, she recognized that what had happened wasn't her fault, and doing what she'd needed to do to stay alive had made her a stronger person.

Surprisingly, something good had come out of the situation.

She now knew that she could handle anything life threw

at her, even the loss of the people who had become her family.

She glanced down at her phone, wondered if she should call Mike, then found herself getting annoyed that he'd given up so easily.

Maybe he wasn't the man she thought he was...

She sighed. Of course, he was. It was her own self-doubts, her own bruised ego that was harping at her now.

Then she was distracted by the accused being brought into the courtroom, the judge returning to the bench, the jurors filing in...and then thankfully, the guilty verdict. By the time the sentence was announced, she was already closing the book on that chapter of her life.

Texting Abby to arrange for therapy—surprise, surprise, her brilliant sister had been right.

Planning where to go from here—definitely Mike's to see if he still wanted her, to see if he hadn't changed his mind about her being around the twins.

When she stepped out of the courthouse into the sunshine reflected off the blinding white snow, her parents walked on either side of her and protected her from the reporters. Yet when the reporters parted to allow her through, she glimpsed a familiar looking truck, then a familiar looking man holding a sign that said *Marry us, Jane*.

The twins each held a corner of the sign and if she hadn't already been hooked, their hopeful expressions would have reeled her in.

Beside her, Barbara Watts said, "Well, will you look at that, Walter. Seems like we're about to be blessed with the sweetest grandchildren ever." She nudged Jane in the ribs. "Not that I'll ever give up on the dream of a half dozen more, so don't think I'm letting you off the hook, honey."

Jane wiped at the moisture gathering in the corner of one eye, afraid to get her hopes up too high. "Oh Mom, there's plenty of time for babies. Maybe this is a ploy to give the journalists something else to focus on. Mike's kind of thoughtful and sweet that way."

Her dad urged her down the steps with a gentle hand against the middle of her back. "That boy always did wear his heart on his sleeve, so if you're going to break it, do it gently. Better yet, just marry the boy and be a good mama to his little girls."

"Oh Dad." She sniffled, then had to wipe her other eye and accept a tissue from her mom.

Off to the side of Mike and the twins, Abby stood, and despite her sour expression, offered support with a definite thumbs up.

Meanwhile, the reporters were going crazy. With a whole new story underway, it seemed the murder trial and outcome had been forgotten while cameras clicked and people spoke into microphones or texted the story back to the office.

Jane ignored them all while she cautiously made her way down the courthouse steps and stopped a few feet away from the man she loved and his precious family. He quirked one masculine brow at her and simply said, "Come home, Jane. You belong with us."

Then he released the sign into the girls' hands and approached her, love and tenderness and forever in his gaze. A few inches away, he stopped, giving her the choice whether or not she wanted to take that final step.

And with a deep sigh and a happy squeal, she launched herself into his arms and kissed him, ignoring the cameras and the crowd and the past.

The twins began to cheer in their outside voices.

When they finally came up for air, Mike smiled down at her. "I love you."

"I love you too."

And from here on out, that was all that mattered.

EPILOGUE

One year later...

Jane woke to the sound of childish giggles, and realizing she'd slept through the entire night, jerked totally awake. Then she heard a man's chuff of laughter and she relaxed.

Mike.

With a happy sigh, she turned on the bedside lamp, got out of bed to use the bathroom, splash some water on her face, and fluffed her hair. As she climbed back into bed, she heard the twins race down the hallway.

They burst into the bedroom and seeing that she was awake, shouted, "Good morning, Jane."

"Good morning, my lovelies."

They climbed onto the bed, slid under the blankets, cuddled against her, and she hugged them tight.

Lisa wrinkled her nose, and held it between her thumb and index finger. "Ben left Daddy a big deposit."

Jane laughed and gave her an extra squeeze.

On the other side, Laura twisted a lock of Jane's hair around her finger and asked, "Can we stay home from school today to help you and Daddy with Ben?"

"No, but it's almost Easter break. You can help then." And she gave the older-by-two-minutes twin a big squeeze too.

Then she heard the scuff of Mike's sock feet against the flood boards, and he walked through the open doorway, tall, handsome, happy…carrying their precious newborn son in his arms. The love in his eyes was as steadfast and solid as the man coming her way.

"Good morning, Mama. I brought you a little someone." The baby in his arms started squirming. "And this someone has an appetite like his sisters."

The twins gave her room to take the baby from their father, and she lifted her face for his kiss. As he transferred the baby into her arms, he kissed her, then climbed onto the bed and sprawled out on his side, one hand supporting his head, his rapt attention on the opening of her nightgown.

She blushed and laughed. "Isn't this getting old?"

His eyes twinkled. "Are you kidding. It's almost my favorite time of the day."

Laura settled into his chest as she too watched the process of Jane feeding the baby. "Daddy, what is your favorite time of the day?"

He gave her a noisy kiss. "Why, it's when you girls get off the bus and we're all back together again."

Lisa patted him on the cheek and smiled. "Good answer." Then she snuggled in beside her sister.

She was calmer these days, not so prone to going into hyperdrive.

Jane's cell phone whistled. Mike reached over her, grabbed it, and glancing at the screen, held it out to her. "It's Abby."

She smiled back at him. "What does she want?"

His gaze drifted from her face, down to the bare mound of her breast where the baby suckled noisily. His eyes grew hot enough to scorch her, before he blinked and asked, "What was the question?"

Lisa rolled her eyes. "Baby Ben make Daddy daft."

Jane laughed. The twins were just finishing grade one and they were both little reading machines. "Did you learn a new word at school, sweetie?"

"Silly, foolish, simpleton." She reached behind her head, and cupped Mike's cheeks with a huge grin on her face. "*Daddy!*"

Mike bent and blew a noise into her neck. "Someone is getting brussels sprouts for supper."

Laura wrinkled her nose and focused on Jane. "When will Ben be old enough to eat real food?"

Exchanging a look with her husband—she knew exactly why the older twin wanted to know, so she could feed him all her unwanted food—she replied. "Not for a long time, honey."

Then she refocused on the text. "So what does Abby want this early in the morning?"

He silently read the text, a frown forming between his brows. "She wants to know when you're going to come to your senses and dump the loser." He whistled and glanced up at her. "Still? I thought by now she'd be over her dislike of me."

"Abby doesn't like anyone with a—" She cleared her throat and wiggled her eyebrows as she glanced down at his crotch.

Lisa covered her mouth with her hands and sang, "*Penis!*"

Mike ruffled her hair. "We don't use that word around other adults, right?"

She uncovered her mouth and grinned up at him. "Right, Daddy."

Laura grabbed a tissue and leaned forward to wipe some milk drool from the edge of the baby's mouth. "How come Aunt Abby doesn't like men?"

"Someone she loved very much broke her heart and she never got over it."

"Sad," the girls said in unison.

Mike shook his head. "Good luck to the unlucky bastard who someday falls in love with her. He's going to have his hands full."

"Aww, come on, admit it. You love my sister."

"I do, but what's the fun in letting her know that?" His cell beeped, and he glanced down at the screen, then rolled off the bed, somehow taking Lisa with him so by the time he was standing on his feet, she was giggling in his arms. He released her. "Kiss Jane and Ben goodbye, girls. It's time to catch the bus."

There was a flurry of activity and kisses and one armed hugs, and protecting Ben so he didn't get squished in the process. And as the girls raced from the room, Mike strolling along behind them, he paused at the door and gave her a tender smile filled with the promise of forever. "Be back in a few. Don't go anywhere."

As he turned and disappeared down the hallway, Jane focused on the wide-eyed baby in her arms. He was clinging to her nipple with his mouth, the suckling motion momentarily paused as he listened to the sound of his sisters leaving for school. And as the door banged shut and the house turned quiet, he turned his blue-eyed gaze on her face and resumed feeding.

Jane laughed softly and stroked the back of her fingers against his soft cheek. "Don't worry, sweetheart, you'll get used to the commotion around here and one day soon, you'll be part of it."

Life had turned sweet for both Jane and Mike and their growing family.

Several months ago, Harley and Gage had been blessed with a sweet little boy, a cousin for Laura and Lisa and Ben. And Sara's Emma, at nearly two years old, was smart and precocious like her mother.

A few minutes later, she heard the click of the back door. Then Mike was climbing back onto the bed. He sat shoulder to shoulder with her and together they watched their baby suckle, the motions growing intermittent as his eyelids grew heavy and finally drifted shut.

Mike's low voice awoke a hunger deep in her belly. "We're officially outnumbered."

She turned her head so she could look at her handsome husband. "You love it."

His eyes warmed with sweet tenderness. "I love you too."

And as he leaned in to kiss her, Jane smiled against his mouth.

This was their forever time.

THE END

ABOUT THE AUTHOR

Sheila Seabrook writes love stories with heart and humor from her home on the beautiful Canadian prairies. Her romantic books are filled with smart, sassy women, hot men who love them, and a wild assortment of family members guaranteed to try to steal the show.

When Sheila's not writing, she can usually be found in her favorite chair doing research (code for reading romance books) or devising multiple excuses to avoid cooking, laundry, housework, and shoveling the snow. She does, however, love to shop for flowers in the spring, and spends copious hours digging in the dirt to plant them (although her marriage contract clearly stipulates that the man of the house must pull the weeds).

Her mission in life is to give readers emotional romantic stories and unforgettable characters, a relaxing treat for the end of the day. And if she can help them escape the laundry pile, she's totally on board.

Find out more about Sheila at www.sheilaseabrook.com and make sure to join her monthly newsletter to receive exclusive updates, free stories, and more!

4313414 33674

Made in the USA
Columbia, SC
10 September 2017